The Catalysts

The Catalysts

A Novel

Joseph Guzzo

RESOURCE *Publications* · Eugene, Oregon

THE CATALYSTS
A Novel

Resource Publications
An Imprint of Wipf and Stock Publishers
199 W. 8th Ave., Suite 3
Eugene, OR 97401

www.wipfandstock.com

PAPERBACK ISBN: 979-8-3852-3693-0
HARDCOVER ISBN: 979-8-3852-3694-7
EBOOK ISBN: 979-8-3852-3695-4

VERSION NUMBER 11/22/24

For Maria and Joseph III, my favorite savages

"The smallest feline is a masterpiece"

—Leonardo da Vinci

Acknowledgements

It was a wet, miserable Saturday morning when Red entered our lives. Joe's soccer game was stopped on account of the weather, so we took a trip to a nearby cat shelter. A charismatic orange-and-white chap caught our eye, and he had found his forever home. Smart, loving, but with a penchant for mischief, Red was a wonderful and entertaining pet for 13 years.

Fatty came along a few years later, and while we never did find out the story behind her hobbled leg, I've done my best to fill in the blanks in the story you're about to read.

My furry muses may be gone, but their stories and spirits endure.

I'd like to thank Matthew Wimer and the team at Resource Publications and Wipf & Stock for making this book a reality and for always being there to answer my questions along the way.

Dina Smith, my longtime boss and friend, thanks for being an early reader and for allowing me to include you in these pages.

Brendan McLaughlin, your eagle-eyed copy-editing skills have again been invaluable.

Michael Ayoob and Brad Powell, thanks again for your insights and encouragement along the way. Sadly, your football-prognostication skills have not improved one whit over the years. Or perhaps they have, but it's my acknowledgments page and my reality, delusional as it may be.

Mom, Tom, Amy, Angelica, Anthony, Uncle Ray, and Jim—I can't imagine my life without any of you in it.

One of the many joys of parenting for me was reading to you, Joseph. I treasure those hours we spent lost in imaginary worlds, and this book is my attempt to create such a work for others to enjoy.

Maria, 33 years and counting, and I'm still in love with you. Thank you for being my best friend.

And to the brave immigrants in my family who came to these shores armed with little more than their dreams, I am forever in your debt and will forever stand on your shoulders. Your spirit infuses my life in ways you can't imagine.

ORVILLE WAS LONELY. HE was never alone—there was endless fighting and hissing to annoy and sometimes entertain him—but, as usual, he was lonely. If even one of his remaining mates had the gift, the shelter would have been almost bearable.

He spent his days bestowing names on the others: Sunset, who was orange like him, but ornery and prone to low growling; Coal and Midnight, sweet-tempered black cats whom Orville assumed were brothers; Jerkface McBully, a tuxedo cat who had a habit of eating everyone else's food.

There were currently 83 cats in the shelter. Orville had names for all of them. And while he was always happy when one of his pals was chosen and whisked away, his little heart broke every time he was overlooked.

"Why not me?" he would think. "I'm a handsome bloke. I'm friendly. And if only they knew . . ." He was right. He was handsome and friendly. His orange-and-white coat was shiny. His striped tail was long and complemented his lean, athletic body. Yet, every time, he was disregarded. It had been months now. Would he ever get out of this place?

He became tired of the drill. The humans would look around. They often had a mini-human with them. The cats instinctively knew it was showtime. Even Sunset would hide his nastiness and pretend he was house-worthy. Orville would play it cool and try to be his handsomest. Yet they'd pick Smarmy, the smug calico. Yeah, she was cute, Orville would admit. Or Mr. Whiskers, a dude with exceptionally long whiskers. Sure, he was unique. Orville understood.

And whenever a family picked Sunset, Orville wanted to yell, "Ha! Bad move! See you back here in a week!"

And every time he was proved right. Sunset was a good-looking cat, but he made four return trips to the shelter. Let's just say he wasn't an ideal pet. And each time he returned, he grew a little bit meaner.

"He's a lifer," Orville would say to himself while often giving Sunset wide berth.

At least the volunteers were nice to him. They were nice to everyone. Orville often dreamt that one of them would break him out of here. But he knew from their conversations that they all had cats of their own. There was no room for Orville.

The volunteers left at 5:00 and wouldn't return till 8:00 the following morning. The nights and early mornings were so long. Orville tried sleeping the time away, but it was always difficult with the constant hissing and running that would fill the dark hours.

There were even a handful of cats who had managed to burrow under the drop ceiling and take up residence there. They would look down on the others, apparently hoping to spot a gazelle or unattached zebra.

Orville had to admit he found this entertaining. Every night they would shoot across the shelving units, where food and supplies were kept, reach the top of one of them, and disappear into the ceiling, only to emerge a few seconds later, spying down on everyone else as if they were getting away with a jewel heist. About an hour later, they'd casually jump down, acting as though they had acquired secret knowledge.

Eventually, he'd hunker down with Coal and Midnight, dreaming of his forever home and the joy it would surely bring him.

SHE WAS ON ALERT. It felt good to get out of the cold, but she knew that the two-legged was home. And she didn't want a repeat performance of what happened the last time he found her hiding in his basement.

As fearful as she was of another encounter, she just couldn't bear being outside on such a cold night. And since the two-legged hadn't fixed the hole in his window well—or, more likely, wasn't even aware of its existence—she figured it was worth the risk.

It was easy to hide amidst the debris of the two-legged's mess of a cellar. As long as he slept and didn't venture down here, she could get some much-needed rest before escaping back out at sunrise.

Her life was hard, and it took all her energy just to stay alive. If she wasn't hunting or scrounging through the occasional garbage can in search of tasty morsels, she was trying to find a safe place to sleep. And she was always vigilant—for territorial cats or other animals or the ill-tempered two-leggeds, some of whom seemed to hold such disdain for her type.

Occasionally, she would come across a house and see one of her own sitting in a window. The first time she encountered such a sight, she almost fainted. The cat in the window looked so calm and well-fed. And warm! Maybe not all the two-leggeds were so awful. But she knew some of them were. She had to keep up her guard.

Yet she wondered. How do I end up like one of those window cats? Do I walk up to a house and start scratching on the door? What if that angers the two-legged? Do I jump up on a windowsill and get the attention of the cat? Maybe housecats don't want to share the good life. Do I make a ruckus outside in the wee hours of the morning? No, that's probably not a good idea.

Her days were monotonous yet spiked with fear. She was always hungry and often cold. Any attempt to strike up a friendship with a fellow cat never worked, even though she was a sweetheart. She was on her own, surviving by her wits.

Still, that night, she slept well. The two-legged barely made a noise, and the old rug she found and promptly climbed beneath provided the warmth she coveted. She dreamt of becoming one of those happy house-cats in a home filled with nice two-leggeds. They would all be friends, and she would have all the food and attention she ever dreamt of. And she would have happy, fearless sleep every night.

Alas, the sun rose, and she had to face her harsh reality: Undoubtedly, the two-legged would come down to the cellar at some point, and so she stretched, doffed the rug, and hobbled out the way she had entered, with the two-legged being none the wiser.

The day was barely warmer than the night had been, but at least it was sunny. Maybe she would find a warmish spot to have a nap or come upon some discarded two-legged food or a slow rodent. It was the best she could hope for. And when the sun set, she would probably sneak back into the two-legged's basement. As risky as that was, it was better than dealing with mean cats, raccoons, and whatever else the cold night had in store for her.

FRIDAY HAD LED A good existence. She came into Victor and Claudia's life through a coworker of Vic's, who discovered the frail stray one morning in her backyard and asked if someone was interested in taking home a cat.

Vic and Claudia had recently moved into their home and had been considering acquiring a pet. The story of the scared kitty struck a nerve in Vic, and the little tuxedo cat had found herself a home.

For 16 years, she had been their faithful pal, always happy to see them when they came home from work and always happy to snuggle on an available lap. Though she wasn't crazy about visitors—every knock at the door prompted her to shrink herself an inch lower to the ground before scurrying upstairs to take refuge under her peoples' bed—she adapted well when baby Luca arrived some years ago. She instinctively knew that the boy was family and that he was to be treated as such.

She endured his toddler years, when he would grab her tail and giggle. Vic or Claudia would tell Fri that Luca didn't know any better and admonish her not to lash out. And though she didn't understand the words they were saying, she could tell by their loving tone that the little person meant no harm and that perhaps the best course for her would be to keep her distance.

Blessedly, Luca wasn't two forever, and she eventually grew to love the boy as much as she did the boy's parents.

Now, though, the end of her life was near. The vet said that she was terminally ill and that nothing could be done for her. Her humans made sure she was as comfortable as she could be in her final months, and one Sunday morning, her eyes refused to see another day.

Months passed. They all missed their little friend, and every time any of them reached the bottom step heading into their home's foyer, they would instinctively pause, expecting Fri to fly across their path, as she so often did with such exquisite timing each day of her life.

5

While Vic had promised Luca that come spring they would think about getting another cat, when spring arrived, Vic was half-hoping that Luca had forgotten about the promise because he wasn't sure he was quite ready to replace Friday.

Luca was too sweet a boy to directly ask his parents about getting a new pet, but he mentioned missing Friday enough that Vic got the hint.

So, one Saturday morning, after Luca's wet, muddy soccer game in April of 2012, the three of them stopped by an animal shelter five minutes from where Luca's game had been. Vic had made the appointment a few days before.

"Where are we going, Dad?"

"Well, Luca, your mom and I thought it might be time to take home a new friend . . . if that's okay with you."

Luca's smile answered affirmatively, and the three of them, soaked and cold, were about to cross paths with a cat who would forever change all their lives.

IT WAS WINTERTIME. SUNDOWN came early, and soon the stars would put on their beautiful show. But a clear night meant a cold night, and so she made the small trek back to the nasty two-legged's basement, where the rug she snuggled under the night before was in the same place, as if awaiting her arrival.

She quickly dashed under it and immediately fell into blissful sleep. She had spent hours on the hunt and was successful enough only to stave off complete hunger. And she barely had found time to nap—or a sunny spot in which to do so—before the sun called it a day. Her sleep was so deep, in fact, that she never heard the two-legged descending the creaky staircase, and she had no idea her tail was extending outside the rug.

She didn't hear him when he yelled, "So, you're back, huh?!"

She didn't hear him when he swore loudly and picked up the nearest heavy object, which again was a rusted candleholder.

Fortunately, the rug absorbed most of the candleholder's impact, and before the two-legged had time to reload, the brown tabby bulleted out the window and back into the cold night. In the minute she paused to assess what had happened, she heard him nailing an old piece of wood into place to cover the hole that was her escape from the cold.

The canopy of stars gave her little solace, but at least she was alive. Now, though, she would have to find a new nighttime hiding spot. Maybe it was time to take a bold step and find a way to become one of those housecats that she came across every once in a while.

How did that even happen, she wondered again. And sometimes she would catch a glimpse of a two-legged with a cat, which completely confused her. The two-leggeds were mean, right? But at least some of them were nice to her kind?

Maybe it was a trick! That had to be it. Her kind were lured into dwellings, and there they became prisoners of the two-legged! And who knows what went on then.

At least she had her freedom. But it was cold. And it was only December. It would be frigid for months. Food was scarce. Her semi-safe night spot was no longer safe.

The poor girl found a pile of leftover leaves and nestled beneath them.

The sun would soon awaken, and with it would bring the hopes of a new day and a better life.

IT WAS SATURDAY, WHICH meant more visitors. Orville tried hard to not get his hopes up, but he couldn't help himself. It was around 9:00 when the humans started milling about.

"Oh, isn't he adorable!" said one of them, looking at Snowball, a perfectly cute, little ball of white with a fat tail. Snowball was as good as in. "Good for her," thought Orville.

Sunset was getting the once-over from a middle-aged couple. Orville sighed to himself. "Don't do it, folks," he wanted to say. "You look like nice, orderly people. You'll feel bad when you come back in three days with Sunset in tow."

Orville felt eyes on him. The eyes belonged to a tousle-haired 11-year-old. His heart started to flutter. He heard the boy talking to his father.

"Dad," said Luca, "what about this one?"

Orville wanted to leap into the man's arms but thought better of it.

"Hmm . . . he is a handsome fella, isn't he?" said Vic.

"Yes. Yes, I am," thought Orville. "But that's only the beginning of my charms."

"Excuse me," said Vic to one of the volunteers. "What can you tell us about this one?"

"Oh, that's Orville, sir. He's got quite the personality. Someone brought him and his mother in as strays about three months ago. A nice couple adopted his mom but only had room for one cat. He's a keeper. You can pick him up if you'd like."

And Vic did just that. And Orville looked deeply into Vic's eyes, hoping to make a connection.

"Why, hello," said Vic. "What do you think, guys?"

Claudia and Luca nodded in assent.

Orville's little heart just about exploded from his chest. He was going home! To a family! And they seemed nice. He wished he could thank all the volunteers who were kind to him these months. And he wished he could have said goodbye to his pals. But before he knew it, he was in a carrier sitting in the backseat of a car next to Luca.

"He's not an Orville, Mom," said Luca.

"I was thinking the same thing, honey."

Vic chuckled. "Well, Luca, it's your job to name him. Let him get accustomed to his new home. His true name will emerge soon enough."

"Call me anything you want," thought Orville. "Ham Sandwich. Football. Spatula. Honestly, I don't care. I'm going home!"

The 20-minute trip was a blur. Suddenly, he was free from his carrier and able to check out his new surroundings. There were so many new smells. But the first thing he did was walk up to Luca and give him a nudge. Luca giggled.

"I think he likes you, buddy," said Vic.

"Like him?" Orville wanted to shout. "I adore this kid. He was my ticket out of that place." And for a moment, Orville thought about the pals he left behind. He hoped they'd catch the lucky break that he was experiencing. He wished there was something he could do to help them. But right now there were rooms to explore and smells to investigate and tall bookshelves to reach the tops of.

He followed his people as they showed him around. They pointed out the little bed they bought him. They placed it next to the fireplace in the living room. He didn't know such a thing existed. They showed him Luca's room, and Orville couldn't help but notice what a comfy bed Luca had. And then he snuck into the master bedroom and saw the size of Vic and Claudia's bed. And in the living room, there was a couch and a sofa. There were so many comfortable places for a nap. Orville felt almost overwhelmed.

And don't even get him started on the windows. Big windows with comfy windowsills in the dining room and living room. And in the kitchen? A greenhouse window, which meant not only a place to spy the world from but also a toasty spot for a nap whenever he grew bored viewing outside.

After he was done daydreaming about his greenhouse-window naps, he noticed his food and water bowls. They were his own. He no longer had to share food and water with the other cats. And the food? It smelled so much better than what he was used to. He took a bite. It tasted better, too. He started to feel guilty again, thinking about the plight of his old pals, but those feelings instantly dissipated when he saw a mouse scamper across the floor.

He instinctively pounced on it and immediately realized that it wasn't a mouse but a mouse-shaped object that smelled of something delicious. He clutched it with his front paws while clawing at it with his back paws and chomping down on it.

"I think our new friend just discovered the joys of catnip," said Claudia.

Catnip? Orville had never heard of it, but whatever the humans called it, it was heavenly. He spent several minutes batting the toy mouse around and then jumping on it. And then he jumped on the loveseat and napped with hardly a care in the world.

When he awoke, he was startled to see Luca six inches from him, staring directly into his eyes. Orville jumped back, which made Luca laugh. Orville quickly remembered where he was and then casually stretched all his legs before resuming the assault on his catnip mouse. He then decided to put on a show for his people.

He took a few quick laps from living room to kitchen and back and then, without a warning, propelled himself through the air and gracefully landed atop a tall bookshelf in the corner of the living room.

"Orville's quite the athlete," said Vic.

"He's not an Orville, Dad."

"Well, actually, he kinda is."

Luca gave his father a curious look.

"Orville and Wilbur Wright were brothers who invented the airplane, Luca. And our four-legged Orville sure knows how to fly."

Luca processed this new bit of knowledge for a minute but then shook his head. "He's still not an Orville, Dad."

"Okay, well, let the rebranding be your project, then."

"What's 'rebranding,' Dad?"

"It's a fancy word for giving something a new name or trying to give it a new image. Like, say, a car company is associated with old people, right? Maybe they'll go out and get some young, popular singer to endorse their product so that it seems cooler."

"Is rebranding a form of lying, Dad?"

"Well, that may be a bit harsh, but it's sort of . . ."

"Lying-adjacent, dear?" asked Claudia.

"What's 'adjacent,' Mom?"

Orville watched from his perch as this back-and-forth continued. Again, he wasn't concerned about his name. Orville was fine. Eraser. Nosebleed. Ceiling Fan. Honestly, he didn't care what his people came up with. He was home, and life was good.

LIFE WAS ANYTHING BUT good for our outside feline. The good news, though? It was spring. The bad news? Winter had been harsh. She was hungry. And while the nights wouldn't be nearly as cold, she decided she had had enough. It was time to take a bold step.

She embarked on a new path that morning and soon found herself in a backyard and spotted one of those window cats. He was orange and half asleep. She took a few cautious steps forward. No reaction. She climbed up the back-porch steps. Still nothing. She took a playful swat at a Wiffle ball lying on the porch. The orange cat awoke. The two of them immediately locked eyes. They knew.

"What's it like? Are you safe?" she asked.

"I've been here two weeks. It's awesome," said Orville. "I used to be like you, till someone took me to a shelter."

"What's a shelter?"

"It's a place where kindhearted humans take us so that other kindhearted humans can give us homes."

"What's a hum—oh, the two-leggeds are called humans. Got it! But there are no kindhearted two-leggeds."

"Sure there are," said Orville.

"No, they're mean," she insisted.

"And now I'm the King of Neptune!" yelled Vic, as he chased a laughing Luca through the dining room while brandishing a foam sword.

"Yeah . . . not all of them," said Orville. "Anyway, what's your story?"

"I'm not sure I have one. I've been outside for a while. I'm always hungry. You're the first cat I've ever met who's like me. I don't have any cat friends. I don't have any friends. And the two-leggeds are mean."

"Do you have a name?"

"No. Do you?"

"Well, apparently, it's in the process of being rebranded."

"What's that mean?"

"I have no idea. But you look hungry, friend. Let me get my humans' attention."

And with that, Orville shoved the nearest picture frame to the floor.

The clattering was loud enough for Vic and Luca to stop playing.

"Why'd you do that, buddy?" asked Vic, as he put the frame back on the windowsill.

"Dad, look."

"Oh, what do you know? Another cat."

Orville meowed.

"What's that? You think we should give him some of your food?"

Orville meowed louder.

Vic grabbed a plastic takeout container and filled it with Orville's dry food. But by the time he reached the back porch, the skittish cat had scurried to the yard's back gate.

"It's okay, friend. You don't have to be afraid."

She wasn't afraid. She was terrified. Maybe this was all an elaborate setup and the orange cat was behind the entire evil operation. But, boy, she was hungry.

She waited until Vic was back in the house and took cautious steps toward the sustenance.

As she was devouring the food, Orville ever so lightly tapped on the window. She looked up at him. He nodded at her and whispered, "Stay on the porch. It's safe here. And there's plenty more where that came from."

She didn't trust him, but she figured it wouldn't hurt to take a nap under the porch furniture and reassess things after she awoke.

She woke up confused but immediately remembered where she was and promptly resumed eating.

"Hey," said Orville. "You're still here."

"I don't really have anywhere else to go."

"Well, I don't think the humans would mind if you made their porch your home."

"Why should I trust you?"

"I suppose you shouldn't. It's entirely up to you. But I'm telling you. My humans will feed you. And who knows? Maybe you'll wind up inside with me."

"How do I know you're not a prisoner? Or part of some evil plot to kidnap me?"

"Well, for starters, I have my own bed to sleep in. I rarely do, of course, because the humans' beds are even better. And don't forget the couches. And don't even get me started on that window in the kitchen"—

"Enough! Your words could be nothing but lures. I don't trust you. You could be some weirdo living with a bunch of crazy two-leggeds."

She stopped herself and thought she may have offended her potential friend.

"I'm sorry. It's just—"

"Don't apologize. I was you once. My mom and I . . ." Orville couldn't finish his thought. "Just stay put . . . please?"

She had a choice to make. She could continue her wandering and find something great. Or something nightmarish. Or she could hang out here for a while and see what transpired. She was near a house but not inside it. If one of the two-leggeds—or the four-legged—turned out to be a monster, she could scurry away to freedom. And, after all, that food was pretty tasty.

"Okay, I'll stay . . . for now."

"Good! And I'll do my best to let my humans know you're around."

And for the next several weeks, that's how it played out. Orville would meow loudly while sitting at the dining-room window, and Vic would proceed to bring food outside to his timid friend, who would make a quick dash to the furthest reach of the yard as soon as she heard the door open.

Vic would return inside, and by the time he put the food bag back atop the fridge, she would be happily munching away.

Vic would tap the back-door window. "I see you, silly!" She would look up for a second and do her best to see if he had kind eyes. But she would look away before she could make an assessment. She sort of thought maybe he did. But what if it was all a ruse? Sure, they ply her with food and sweet talk and then, blammo, she's in a cat dungeon. Best to keep her guard up a while longer.

IT TURNED OUT THAT Orville was quite the handful. Endlessly energetic, and with a penchant for shoving objects to the ground (Crashy is good; liquid is awesome. Crashy and liquid? Be still, my heart was Orville's reasoning) he made for a challenging housemate.

But he would spend hours cuddled on a lap or snuggled against one of his humans in bed, and he would listen attentively when Vic would read to Luca every morning before school. He would stretch out on Luca's play rug and stare at Vic. There were times Vic convinced himself Orville was truly taking in Harry, Ron, and Hermione's latest adventure or finding out what the Pevensie children were up to, but he dismissed it as crazy thoughts.

One evening, the family was playing Monopoly, and Orville felt left out. So, naturally, he took a running leap from the dining room and dove into the middle of the board, scattering the game pieces throughout before landing on his favorite perch atop the bookshelf.

Before Vic or Claudia could reprimand Orville, Luca said, "Orange Flame."

"What, honey?" asked Vic.

"He's an Orange Flame. That's his name. He's fast, and he's orange."

Vic and Claudia exchanged a quick glance.

"'Orange' is kind of an odd word," Vic started to say as Claudia gathered the red and green monopoly properties that Hurricane Orville had displaced.

As he saw what his mother was doing, he then said, "Okay, well, how about Red Flame, then?"

And they all exchanged glances because they knew it was perfect. Even Orville, now Red, knew it was right, as he climbed down to rejoin the family.

"I don't know what we're going to do about you, Orville—pardon me, Red Flame—but the boy has given you quite the perfect name," said Vic.

Red meowed, and the family resumed its game, all keeping a wary eye on Red in case he decided to disrupt everything again.

The next morning, the outside cat was in a deep sleep and didn't hear Vic approaching. But when the food hit her bowl, she darted off the porch and headed to safer territory at the bottom of the yard, but not before Vic noticed her malformed front left leg.

"Oh, you poor thing," he said. "How did that happen?"

She heard every word. It started to occur to her that he might have kind eyes. Instead of darting to the gate, she took a few steps toward him and looked directly into his eyes. Yep, they were kind. But she still had to be cautious. She wanted to yell, "A two-legged did this! And you're a two-legged. And maybe you know him. And—and—and I don't know what to think!"

Vic took a step in her direction, and she took two quick steps backward.

"Okay, buddy. Look. I'm giving you food, and I'm going back inside. But we made progress, didn't we?"

Progress for what, though, she wondered. "Am I on my way to becoming a loved family member? Or is the mean two-legged lurking in their basement, armed with a box of candleholders and just waiting to use me as target practice?"

As much as he loved his humans, Red's favorite time of the day was when he could safely chat with his cat pal. Luca was at school, Claudia was at work, and though Vic worked from home, he would spend hours in his office, doing whatever it is humans did to keep the lights on and the kitty bowls filled with food.

Red tapped on the dining-room window, and up jumped his friend.

"Turns out I have a name," said Red. "Red Flame."

"What had they been calling you?" she asked.

"That's not important. But I like Red Flame."

"How did they decide on that?"

"Because I was being awesome."

She rolled her eyes. "I suppose you want to tell me the details."

"It was no biggie. I just did my usual running through the house and landing on top of the bookshelf in a single bound."

"Hm. Jumping's not really my thing, Red."

"Yeah, I figured. You're more earthbound. Have you given any more thought to joining me on the other side of this window?"

"Your human has kind eyes. What about the other two?"

"Oh, they're monsters!" Red yelled.

She jumped back and nearly rolled off the windowsill. Not having to chase for her food and having a steady place to sleep made her plumper than she'd ever been.

"Dang it, Red. What's wrong with you?"

"Come on. They're just as nice as Papa."

"Papa?"

"Yep, that's my name for him—not that he's aware, of course. Papa, Mama, and the Boy."

"You're smitten."

"You would be, too, if you came in."

"I'm giving it serious thought, okay? Let me have a few more inter-actions with the two-legged."

"Fine," said Red before settling down for a windowsill nap.

A few minutes later, Vic entered the kitchen to make himself lunch. He peered out the back door and was surprised to see the porch cat star-ing right at him.

"You hungry, buddy? Give me a second, all right?"

She kept staring. Vic felt as though he were being scrutinized. He chuckled, grabbed the cat-food bag, and paid her a visit.

She didn't run away. He couldn't believe it.

He took a step toward her food bowl. She didn't start walking back-ward. He reached down and filled her bowl. She took a step toward the bowl.

He didn't move, and she began to eat.

"Hey, buddy, what are you going to do if I reach out my hand?"

He did as promised, and she sniffed his hand. Carefully, he reached up and gave the top of her head a gentle scratch. She moved her head into his hand.

"That's not so bad, is it?"

It's not, she had to admit.

Vic didn't want to press his luck and took cautious steps in retreat as she kept eating. He couldn't wait to tell Claudia and Luca about the progress he'd made.

This two-legged was kind, she decided. And she had no reason not to believe Red Flame about the other two-leggeds. But what if his new name was part of their evil plot? She'd step one paw inside the house, and before she knew it, she'd be whisked downstairs to the dungeon, lit only by wall sconces sporting . . . red flames!

Okay, even she had to admit that seemed pretty ridiculous.

It was a warm spring night. After the sun bid adieu, she hopped into the backyard grass and rolled around for a bit. She saw a grasshopper and tried starting a conversation. It was one-way. She sneakily crept toward a mouse and jumped at him but had no intention of devouring him. She just wanted to be an outside cat one last time. For tomorrow, she would have a family.

AT 7:30 THE NEXT morning, Vic appeared, like clockwork, on the back porch. He was used to the routine. She would scamper down the steps, wait till he filled the bowl, begin to retreat, and then approach the bowl. But after what occurred yesterday, he wasn't sure what would happen.

She was waiting for him. She didn't even appear to be interested in the food. Vic wasn't sure what to do, so he decided to scoop her up in his arms and bring her in. And almost instantly he felt the blood running down his forearms as he watched her flee to the back fence.

They both felt horrible. She wasn't expecting to be grabbed, and she panicked. She was terrified that she had blown maybe the only chance she'd ever have of being loved. And Vic was in physical pain, yes, but, even worse, feared that he had scared her away forever.

He went inside to dress his wounds, and while he did, she tentatively made her way back to the porch. In the mayhem that occurred, Vic had forgotten to fill her food bowl.

"What—what—what was that?!" asked Red. He had witnessed the whole thing.

"I panicked! I feel so stupid. Is the human mad at me? Do I need to leave now? Is he going to throw things at me when he sees me again?"

"Well, he's in pain, and I learned some new vocabulary words, but he's actually worried that you're going to run away now. He's madder at himself than he is at you."

Red heard Vic approaching and quickly pretended he was sleeping. Vic was happy to see that porch cat had returned. He grabbed the food bag and returned to the porch.

As he approached, she took one step back, but Vic instantly put her at ease. "No, don't retreat. I'm not mad. Come eat."

And she did. And he patted her head. And she felt horrible for scratching him. "Tomorrow," she promised herself. "Tomorrow, I go in."

Vic didn't want to press his luck. He wouldn't make any sudden moves. When she wants to come in, she'll let me know, he figured.

So, she spent one more day and night on the back porch. Again, she scampered in the yard and struck up one-way conversations with whomever she could find—a ladybug, a spider, a raccoon disappointed to find that she had eaten all her food. She let the starlight wash over her as she drifted off to sleep, knowing that this night would certainly be her last outdoors.

AT 7:30 THE NEXT morning, Vic appeared, like clockwork, on the back porch, this time with his right forearm bandaged. He was used to the routine. But after what occurred the past two days, he refused to assume what would transpire.

She didn't scamper down the steps. She actually approached him. He extended his hand, as he had done a few days earlier. She reached out and accepted it. He gave her head a tentative pat. She let out a small squeak. He retreated, fearing he might be pressing his luck, and she began to follow him.

"Do you—do you want to come in, buddy?"

She froze. And then she hobbled back to her bowl and began to have breakfast.

Vic sighed. "I'm sorry about yesterday. I wasn't trying to steal you." His voice dropped to a whisper. "But if I were, it's not like the kitty police would arrest me."

Instead of being terrified at Vic's words and having her worst fears vindicated, porch cat sensed that the two-legged with the kind eyes was joking. Vic had passed the final test.

He gave her a good-natured glare and returned inside. Red had been watching the whole scene.

"Dude," said Red.

"Yeah, yeah, I know. And I'm not 'dude,' by the way."

"Do you want an engraved invitation?"

"When the two-legged comes out to feed me tonight, I'll follow him in, okay?"

"You're not going to chicken out?"

"No! And if you're lying to me about the two-leggeds, let me assure you I know tricks as an outside cat that you shelter cats are completely clueless about. What I did to the two-legged yesterday? That's only a small part of my danger arsenal."

"Is—is that a threat?"

"Was it convincing?"

"Not in the least. But it was a good effort."

"Whatever, Red. I'll see you on the other side this evening."

"WELL, SPORT," SAID VIC. "It looks like you're going to have to come up with another name. I think porch cat is ready to come in."

Red's wheels started to turn. He wanted in on the naming, too.

"But don't rush into it," said Claudia. "It'll come to you when the time's right, just like with Reddy."

"Reddy?" thought Red. "Hmm, let's stick with Red, okay?"

When dinnertime arrived, Vic didn't have to do much in the way of convincing. As soon as he opened the side-porch door, there she was. Vic opened the door, and in hobbled porch cat. She was overwhelmed by all the smells—the dinner the humans had eaten, Claudia's perfume, hints of Vic's shaving cream, Red, and a delightful smell emanating from what appeared to be a mouse—but a quick glance yielded no evidence of a mean two-legged armed with candleholders or anything else the least bit menacing.

She was home, and the other two-leggeds were eager to meet her. They all approached but kept their distance, except for Red, who confidently strode up to his new pal and gave her a nudge on the cheek.

The humans purchased a little bed for their new friend, placed right next to Red's. She gave it a quick sniff and then took the same tour Red had months earlier. Like Red, she was overwhelmed at all the excellent sleeping choices, though the greenhouse window was likely outside the range of her jumping capabilities.

She was so happy, she had to fight back tears. These humans were nothing like the mean two-legged, and she couldn't wait to learn everything about them in the days ahead. But it had been a long day, so she climbed into her bed, shut her eyes, and enjoyed the best sleep of her life.

HE AWOKE HUNGOVER. AGAIN. And he was angry—at his condition, at his life, at everything. He plodded into the kitchen and made the same breakfast he had been making since she left—scrambled eggs, three strips of bacon, and burnt toast. The orange juice knocked out the remaining whiskey stench that the toothpaste failed to conquer.

And so his routine began.

He got the paper off the porch. It was the same stories with different names—a car crash on Route 28, an area high school team advanced in whatever sport was in season, couples full of hope, looking their best on their wedding days.

He tossed the paper aside and turned on the TV. Again, it was the same stories with different names—a war over here, an earthquake over there, shiny people selling products no one needed.

It wasn't even 9:30, but he needed his medicine. The first belt always took off the edge. He convinced himself he would wait to have a second until at least noon. He knew he was lying, but maybe if he made his first one strong enough, he'd fall asleep for a few hours, and by the time he'd wake up, it would be past noon.

And that's the plan of action he took. He sat quietly and let the amber liquid work its magic. Sleep came. But so did the dreams. And they always starred her. And she was always young and beautiful and just tantalizingly out of reach.

When he awoke and realized where he was, he grabbed his glass and slammed it against the nearest wall, sat there for a good 15 minutes, and wept into his hands.

And when he composed himself, he realized he had a new problem to deal with: bits of broken glass that covered a good portion of the hallway and into the living room. He walked into the mudroom and felt a hint of shame as he noticed the collection of footballs, Frisbees, and various flying contraptions that he kept from neighborhood kids foolish enough to play near his yard. He snatched a broom and began cleaning up the glass.

"Old Man Bitters." He knew what they called him. Oh, how he hated it! It was so unfair, he would tell himself. They just didn't understand. He had been their age once, though they'd be loath to believe it, and life was all in front of him. He didn't become a mean, old drunk overnight. It took a series of missteps to arrive where he was, on his hands and knees, cleaning up shards of glass, cursing when a shard got the better of him, and thirsting for his next dose.

It's like a hurricane. One does not form in an instant. The stars have to misalign for weeks, and the conditions must be perfectly right yet somehow awfully wrong before its fury is unleashed.

Franklin Betters was a hurricane waiting to happen. Yet he was smart enough to know better, and he knew what he had to do, if only he had the will to do so.

But first he'd watch the early news and see who the new actors were in today's stories.

"Psst! The coast is clear," said Red.

"The coast is clear for what, Red?"

"For anything, dude! Mama's at work, the boy's at school, and Papa's in his office with the door closed."

"Well, what do you normally do?"

"I nap in various places, walk around a bit, have some food, look out a couple windows. But now it's different. I have a pal!"

While porch cat was excited at the prospect of palling around with Red, there was one part of the house she hadn't yet explored.

"That sounds great, Red, but, um, what's behind that door?"

"Oh, that? That's the cellar door. Oh, I get it! You need to use the litter box."

"The what, now?"

"It's our bathroom. You'll figure it out. Go ahead."

Silly as it sounds, there was a bit of hesitation as she gently nudged the door open wide enough for her to fit. She took one cautious step down and then paused.

"Dude, I'd like to play before the boy goes to college. The only thing down there is a washer, dryer, furnace, various toys, and a box full of my pee pucks, assuming no one had the decency to clean it this morning."

"All right, all right." She made it to the bottom of the steps, and it was just as Red had described. She decided that the litter box was an improvement over the backyard. Again, she felt silly thinking the worst.

"Okay, Red, what did you have in mind?"

"Watch this!"

And he took off like a missile, landing atop the bookshelf in seconds. If she was impressed, she didn't let on.

"What? No cheers?"

"You're a cat who jumps, Red. It's not exactly uncommon."

27

"Okay, well, why don't you try it, then?"

"I can't jump like you, Red. You know that."

"Then you should be impressed. Watch this."

And Red then tucked his paw underneath the small lampshade attached to the wall sconce, lifted it up, and watched it clatter to the floor.

The noise was loud enough to alert Vic, who jogged into the living room to see what the problem was.

And what he saw was Red, sitting on top of the bookshelf, trying to look innocent, as though an invisible alien had knocked off the lampshade, and porch cat sitting on the floor, staring at Red.

"She's not impressed, Red," said Vic, before returning the lampshade to its proper place and gently putting Red on the floor beside porch cat.

"I'm busy, pal. Play quietly."

When Vic was out of earshot, porch cat said, "He sees right through you."

"He sees hardly anything," Red said. "He's never without his glasses."

"So . . . what now?" asked porch cat.

"Usually at this time, I eat some dry food and then hop up to the greenhouse window to see the neighbors take their doggos walking. And then I have a nap."

Porch cat sauntered into the kitchen and was embracing Red's agenda by having a second breakfast. She looked up at Red.

"What? It's nice having steady food. You don't know what it's like out there. There were days I went hungry or felt lucky to find a chicken bone in someone's garbage with a bit of meat left on it."

"No, I get it. It's just, well, you're getting a little fatty. Fatty!"

"Why'd you yell that last part, Red?"

"You're Fatty! That's your name."

"I don't think that's nice, Red."

"I'm not being mean. It's just who you are. It's descriptive. The first name our humans came up with for me was Orange Flame, but they decided that orange is kind of an odd word—they're right—so they changed it to Red."

"But your name isn't insulting."

"Meh! Neither is yours. It just feels right."

Porch cat was unsure about her new moniker, but she ignored it. After all, she felt sure the humans would come up with a much better name for her.

As she was just about done eating, she noticed a shiny silver ball coming her way and instinctively pounced on it.

"Whoa! Good reflexes, buddy." Even Red was impressed, though he couldn't bestow a compliment onto his friend at the moment.

No matter which direction Vic rolled his arsenal of foil balls, porch cat pounced, often beating Red to the punch.

After about a minute, Red grew disinterested, but porch cat played on and did her all-star goalie impression repeatedly, never letting Vic get one ball past her.

"Oh, well, back to the salt mines, pals," Vic said as he quickly tossed one more, hoping to prevent a shutout. He failed.

The second he closed his office door, Red jumped off the couch and got right in his new friend's face. "Fatty, how did you do that? Your one leg barely works."

"Food was usually scarce, but when it was available, I knew what I had to do to survive, Red. I may not be able to jump like you, but I have moves of my own."

"We make quite the team, Fatty."

"Are we really sticking with 'Fatty'?"

"It appears that way."

Porch cat sighed. "So, is that a thing Kind Sir does often?"

"'Kind Sir'? Oh, you mean Papa? Yeah, he takes a break from whatever it is he does a few times a day and comes and talks to me or throws me a toy. He tells me his work woes. Sometimes he sings, completely unaware, of course, that I'm not only hearing everything he says but also understanding it. Well, most of it. The work stuff, I don't get."

"He sings?"

"Yeah, when he's in a good mood."

"Does he sing well?"

"No. Just wait. You'll get a taste of his vocal stylings sooner or later."

"Are we lying to our humans, Red?"

"Lying? About what?"

"The fact that we understand most of what they're saying to us and that we can talk."

Red contemplated porch cat's observation and began to speak but was interrupted by his own whirling mind. "I'm—I'm not sure. Is not telling the truth lying?"

They looked at each other.

"Okay, I realize that question sounds ridiculous, Fatty, but how would they react if they learned the truth? They'd pass out. It would upset the balance of nature. Sometimes it's best to not know the truth."

And now it was porch cat's turn to do some contemplation.

"They're going to find out somehow."

"Nah," Red said. "I've been here for months. You'd be amazed how easy it to clam up when they're around. I almost slipped up a few times early on. Don't worry. You'll get used to it."

"But now there's two of us, Red. We're going to slip up. Wouldn't it be better to just come clean?"

"You're probably right, Fatty. In fact, let's go knock on Papa's door. He'll let us in, and I'll say, 'Papa, there's something we've been meaning to tell you.'"

"Okay," said porch cat.

"And then, you pick up the phone and call 911, because Papa might very well smack his head on the desk as he collapses to the floor."

Porch cat realized Red had a valid point and began a different approach until Red cut her off.

"Fatty, it's no big deal. It's our secret. They'll never know. They'll live their regular human lives, we'll talk to each other when we're alone, and the normal order will continue. Trust me."

THE HUMANS WERE FINISHING up dinner, and Luca was staring at porch cat, who was enjoying her own dinner, unaware that an 11-year-old boy was about to unknowingly hurt her feelings while making Red deliriously happy.

"I think I have a name for porch cat," Luca said.

"Well, let's hear it," said Claudia.

Red entered the dining room, boring holes into Fatty with his eyes while saying to himself, "Please say 'Fatty,' boy."

"Fatty," said Luca.

It took every ounce of self-control Red could muster to not burst into hysterics and jump around the house triumphantly. He ducked out of the room as quickly as he could, counting down the minutes till he and Fatty could be alone and he could enjoy the moment.

Similarly, it took every ounce of strength for porch cat not to emit a mournful meow. She was hoping Kind Sir would step in and steer Luca in a different direction.

"Well, Luca, yes, she is on the portly side," Vic said, "but maybe that's not the nicest name, honey?"

"Yes," thought porch cat. "Kind Sir saves the day. I knew it."

"I don't know, Vic," said Claudia. "It's kinda cute. And it's not like she's going to be offended."

"Uh-oh," thought porch cat.

"Fatty!" Vic said. They all chuckled.

Porch cat noted that he said it with kind eyes, and she had to acknowledge that there was no way on Earth they knew that she comprehended every word they were saying. These were good people. She knew that. They gave her a home and love. They would never knowingly hurt her in any way. Yet she would be Fatty going forward. And she would have to process this new information. And she knew Red would be of no assistance.

The humans had gone to bed, and Fatty was sitting in her bed by the fireplace, awaiting Red's arrival. He didn't disappoint.

"F-A-T-T-Y," Red said in a loud whisper. "My goodness, it's like I planted a seed in the boy's head and watched it sprout before my eyes."

"Did you, Red? Is that how it happened?"

"What? Like I snuck into the boy's room at night, climbed up next to his ear, and whispered, "Call porch cat 'Fatty.' It's the right thing to do"?

"That sounds plausible, Red."

"You know, Fatty, I have to admit, it actually does. I'm angry at myself for not doing it. But I didn't—honest. It all happened organically. And hysterically."

Fatty sighed. "It's a stupid name. I hate it."

"It's not a stupid name. The humans think it's cute. They think you're cute. I think you're—well, never mind what I think. It's a done deal."

"I suppose you're right. After all, sticks and stones."

"That's the spirit, Fatty. So, what did break your bone, anyway?"

THE EVENING NEWS WAS over. Even the "feel-good" story at the end of the newscast—about a kid fighting a rare disease while raising money to fight it—did little to brighten his spirits. Only spirits could brighten his spirits, and so he commenced with his favorite pastime.

He thought he heard a noise coming from the basement, so he stumbled downstairs. Everything seemed to be in place. Well, honestly, everything in the basement looked as though a tornado had struck, but it was in the same disorder it had been the last time he stumbled down there. The piece of plywood covering the window-well hole was still in place.

As he made his way back up, he caught a glimpse of the photos that lined the staircase wall. He began feeling a mixture of happiness and rage. The pictures themselves elicited pure joy in him: the birthday parties, the Little League games, graduation pictures, wedding pictures, a permanent representation of the best moments of his life catalogued in chronological order. But then the rage: Where were they? Why didn't they visit or write or call more often?

He smacked one picture right off its nail. He felt empowered as it clattered to the floor and rolled down the steps. Another. And then another. Before he knew it, there were more than a dozen picture frames collected at the bottom platform, and few remained unscathed from chipped wood or broken glass or both.

He punched the wall—he was no longer strong enough for his fist to do any damage—and slammed the cellar door behind him. Well, in his heart, he intended it to be a slam. In reality, it barely closed.

His impromptu workout demanded a drink, and he rewarded himself with a double. It was close to bedtime, anyway, he figured, so why not?

He slumped down into his recliner, drink in hand, and flicked on the TV. The Pirate game was on. Their poor playing fit his foul mood perfectly, and he grumbled himself off to sleep, hoping the whiskey would ease him into comfort.

But it didn't. It never did. It was as if the booze powered the dream machine, and as soon as sleep overtook him, showtime commenced. And his booze movies always starred the same cast: her and them. And they were always so happy. And young and beautiful. These were the worst kind of dreams because they felt so real. If Godzilla shows up in your dream, at some level, you know it's a dream, and your brain quickly dismisses it. "I dreamt I was in English class, and the new student was Godzilla. And he was sitting behind me." Yeah, that dream you immediately dispatch.

But the dreams the old drunk was enduring? There were no monsters. Just his wife and kids and him. And they were ecstatic, so ecstatic that he wanted to jump through his brain and join in their merriment. If only he could, for even a minute. What he wouldn't give for that.

And then he woke up, climbed up to his bedroom, and prayed to God that he could sleep through just one night without seeing any of their faces.

"On cold nights, I was desperate for shelter, Red. While wandering, I came upon a house with a window well. I hopped in, figuring that at least it would protect me from the wind. But then I noticed that a panel in the window was missing. This was even better."

Red unconsciously put his paw on Fatty's, sensing her unease.

"The hole was just wide enough for me to fit through. The basement was a mess, but there were numerous places for me to hide, unnoticed. Or at least I thought."

"Uh-oh. I get the feeling the 'two-legged' is about to show up," said Red.

"Not yet. I thought I had a good thing going, and for a few weeks the cellar was where I spent the nights. And then one night, yes, the two-legged stumbled down the steps. He was yelling about something. And then I guess he saw my tail sticking out from underneath a rug. He charged me, and I got out before we had an encounter."

"Okay, but that doesn't explain your leg." Red gasped. "Did you return?"

"I did, Red. I had no choice. We had a cold spell. It was either take a chance down meanie's cellar or, you know . . ."

"Freeze to death." Red's paw clenched a little harder on his friend. "Oh, Fatty."

"But this time, he pretended he didn't see me. He didn't charge. He was yelling about something. I couldn't really make out what he was saying because he was slurring. But before I could react, he nailed me in the leg with a candleholder. I was somehow able to escape."

"But how did you heal?"

"Time, I guess. But it wasn't easy. I was in pain for weeks, and food was scarce. But the good leg and paw made up for the bad one. I even snuck back in a few more times, I was so desperate when my bones were healing. And I think my tail betrayed me again, because he chased me out. But I got through it. And then I found your porch."

"You mean the dude that did that to you is near us?"

"Well, yeah, he is. But so what? We're safe here."

"Yeah, but he shouldn't feel safe. We ought to pay him a visit."

"Red, that's crazy. What do you propose we do? Escape our home some night, sneak into his, and launch an attack on a very unsuspecting two-legged?"

"Yes! Exactly, Fatty!"

"Red, stop being ridiculous. I'm fine where I am. I never want to look into his mean eyes again, even if he does deserve it."

"See, Fatty? Your wheels are turning."

"My wheels are completely stationary, Red. Good night."

"Good night, pal. We'll get him someday. I promise."

"Okay, Red. Whatever you say. I'm too tired to fight with you."

And with that, the cats went to sleep, safe in their little beds, where they would stay initially to start their night's rest. Eventually, though, they would snuggle up against their humans for extra warmth. Life was good.

LIFE WAS GOOD, EXCEPT when Red would dream about her. And when he dreamt about her, the subject was often their last day together.

It was a regular Saturday at the shelter. And as they had discussed many times—Red's mother had the gift, too—Red and his mother possessed the same wish: to be adopted by nice humans together. But it wasn't meant to be.

"Oh, honey, look at this one," said the young lady to her husband. They seemed like decent folks.

"Adorable," her husband agreed. "Excuse me, miss? What can you tell us about this one?"

"Well, she's a keeper. And that little orange fella? That's her son, Orville. They're very attached. Ideally, they'd be adopted together."

The couple exchanged a glance. "The thing is," the woman said, "we live in an apartment. We're allowed one cat, but I think we'd be pressing our luck with two."

Red and his mom looked at each other. They could only talk to each other when the humans weren't around. Their fates were being decided in front of them, and they had to be silent and let the scene play out.

"I understand," said the volunteer. "Don't worry. I'm sure we'll find Orville a good home, too."

And just like that, Mom was being put in a carrier. She didn't blink the whole time, her eyes set on the love of her life. She figured this was the last time she'd ever see her boy, and she never wanted to forget his handsome face. Red couldn't blink, either. He wanted to yell. He wanted to cry. He could do neither. He could only mouth, "Mom," and she blinked in return, both of them fighting back tears. He stared at her until the happy couple ducked into their car and drove away. He had never felt more alone.

37

Red woke up and sighed. He thought about his mother every day. He was sure she was having a good life, too. That couple seemed like good people. He wondered if his mother thought about him. Of course she did, he reasoned. He'd give up just about anything to see her even one more time. And he could introduce her to Fatty, and they would all have silly-human stories to share. It would be marvelous.

But Red knew it would never happen. He didn't have a clue as to where his mother was. She could be in another state, for all he knew. But he carried her in his heart, and that would have to be enough.

And he knew he and Fatty were lucky. Their biological mothers weren't a part of their lives, but Claudia was a great cat mom. She always shared her food with them. She was a good snuggler. And the love she displayed for Luca always put a smile in Red's heart, for it reminded him of his days with his mom.

Red and Fatty's weekdays began to take on a familiar pattern. Claudia would go to work. Luca would head off to school. And Victor would barricade himself in his office for most of the day, occasionally appearing to give the cats a snack or play with them briefly.

So, it was just another regular Wednesday when Red and Fatty made the biggest error of their young lives.

Their midday snack consumed, they were heading into Luca's room to catch the afternoon sun. The two of them were in mid-conversation—debating the pros and cons of the various cat snacks their humans bought for them—when they laid eyes on Luca. Red let out a "Mrowr," hoping that would give them cover.

"You—you guys talk?" asked Luca, who was home with a sore throat.

"Mrowr," said Red again, hoping against hope that the boy would think he had been dreaming.

"No, I heard you, Red. You said you like the crunchy tuna snacks best, and, Fatty, you said the turkey ones were your favorite."

The cats exchanged glances, unsure of what to do.

"Mrowr," said Red one final time, figuring it couldn't hurt.

"Stop it, Red! I know what I heard."

"Luca," said Fatty.

Luca jumped off his bed and slowly retreated. "What is going on? I-I don't understand."

"Honestly, we don't understand it much better than you do. Fatty and I talk. Not all cats talk. When I was at the shelter, my mom and I were the only two who had the ability."

"It's true, Luca. I encountered numerous cats when I lived outside. None of them talked. But when I met Red, we just knew."

"I'm telling Dad," said Luca.

"No! I-I'm not sure that's the best idea—at least not yet," said Red.

"It might be better if it's our secret, until we figure out what to do and how to tell them," said Fatty.

"But I don't like keeping secrets from Mom and Dad. It's lying."

"Luca, you're a good boy. I understand. But we just don't think your mom and dad are ready to know. We'll know when the time is right," said Red.

Luca didn't know what to think. Ten minutes earlier, he was building a Lego castle and concerned about missing school. And now? He was having a conversation with cats. He knew just what to do.

He dashed down the steps and knocked on his dad's office door.

"Luca, what are you doing?" asked Red. Luca shushed him.

"Come on in, buddy," said Vic.

Luca entered Vic's office, accompanied by his concerned friends.

"Well, I see the whole gang's here. Must be important. Did you guys just come from a meeting?"

Luca chuckled nervously. "Uh, no, Dad. I just wonder if you could check my temperature. I'm feeling kind of warm."

"Oh, honey, that's no good. Let me grab the thermometer."

As soon as Vic was out of earshot, Fatty said, "It's not a fever, pal. But that's good thinking."

"Nope, 98.6, champ. How's your throat feeling?"

"Better. I can go to school tomorrow."

"All right, well, take it easy, and take your assistants with you. I'll be busy for a while. If you're up for it later, we can toss the baseball around."

"Okay, Dad. Thanks."

The three of them scampered away, Luca now content at least that he wasn't having a fever dream involving talking cats.

But he was an 11-year-old boy who was filled with questions the cats couldn't answer.

"How did you realize you could talk?"

"I just could. I assumed all cats could, until I realized none of the other cats around us had the ability, just me and my mom. And when she left, I had no one to talk to," Red said. "And then you showed up and picked me. It was the happiest day of my life, Luca."

Luca smiled. "You looked more alert than all the other cats. And you were staring at me."

"I was at my handsomest because you and your parents seemed like nice people. I was right."

"But, Luca, honey, this is a lot for you to take in. It's a lot for all of us to take in. Promise us you'll tell no one," said Fatty.

"I won't, Fatty, but I don't like it. I mean, my parents have a right to know."

"They do, dear. And I promise you we'll figure something out," said Fatty.

And with that, they left the bewildered boy to return to his Legos and tried to find another toasty spot in which to digest what had just happened.

"How did we not know he wasn't at school, Fatty?"

"I don't know, Red. He usually says goodbye to us. I assumed he had forgotten."

"Well, it doesn't matter now. What are we going to do?"

"I feel wrong dragging him into our secret, Red, but we can't just blurt out to Kind Sir and Mom that we talk. Luca still has an active imagination. He's probably second-guessing that the whole thing even happened."

"What good does that do us?"

"It buys us time, Red. I need a nap. I needed a nap before we got busted. Now I need an extra-long nap."

Red agreed, and they both quickly drifted off in an alternative sunny spot.

The next day, the cats made sure that Claudia was at work and Luca was heading off to school—he said goodbye to them as nonchalantly as he had any other day—before they opened their mouths.

They even took a trip to Vic's office and made sure they heard the clacking of his keyboard before they uttered a word.

"This is more like it, Fatty—no surprises today. We have the run of the house till the boy returns. And since the boy knows our secret, I guess we really have the run of the house till Mama gets home."

"Yeah, that's nice, but we have a problem. How do we tell these lovely people that they're the unwitting owners of talking cats?"

"Don't sweat it, pal. Things have a way of working out. Remember those cold nights when you were shivering outside, unsure of where your next meal was going to come from?"

"Yeah, it's hard to forget those days, Red, try as I may. What's your point?"

"Well, it all worked out, didn't it? Now you're here, and you're safe, and food's available all day long. See? It all worked out."

"Yeah, but it wasn't easy, Red. We could make this simple by knocking on Kind Sir's door and explaining to him the whole situation."

"Fatty, do we have to go through this again? He'll faint on the spot and conk his head on the desk. He'll be unconscious, and though we can talk, we can't operate a phone to call for help. We can't open a window or a door to get help. It'd be a bad scene."

"But—"

"No 'buts,' Fatty dear. Just let it play out. Everything will work out fine. Trust me."

LUCA WAS GLAD TO be back at school. Maybe being around his pals would help him forget that he apparently lived with talking cats, unbeknownst to his parents.

"Luca, you're back!" It was his best friend, Jonathan. "We missed you yesterday, but you didn't miss much."

"Oh, that's good to hear," said Luca, trying a little too hard to sound normal.

"You okay, Luca?"

"Yeah, I'm fine, bro. We'll talk at lunch."

The morning lasted an eternity. Through English, math, and science, all Luca could think about was Red and Fatty. Was it a dream? Maybe the old thermometer no longer worked, and his temperature was actually 106. Maybe if he told Jonathan, it would make more sense, he figured. He couldn't wait for lunch. It was a beautiful spring day. They would get to have recess outside.

"So, what's up, Luca?" asked Jonathan as the two of them headed away from their classmates playing basketball.

"You promise not to laugh?" asked Luca.

"Scout's honor," said Jonathan, lifting three fingers skyward.

"It's—it's nothing," said Luca.

"You can't do that, dude. Out with it."

"Well, it's my cats. I think they talk."

"You mean 'meow-meow' stuff? Yeah, we had a cat that used to talk all the time, too."

"No, I don't mean that exactly."

"What? You mean like English? Like we're talking now?"

There was a pause. Could Luca trust his best friend? He decided he could.

"Yes, they speak in words, but my parents don't know."

Jonathan started to chuckle. "Good one, pal. I suppose they play the piano, too, right?"

Luca didn't break Jonathan's stare.

"Wait. You're serious? Were you out sick with a fever yesterday?"

"That's what I thought, too! But my dad took my temp. It was normal."

"Well, your temp may be normal, but you're not."

"Jonathan, you promised me you wouldn't laugh. You even did the Scout's thing."

"I'm not laughing, bro. I just think you're weird. Cats don't talk."

"That's what I thought until yesterday. Just promise you won't tell anyone else."

"Whatever, dude."

Recess came to an end, the students returned inside, and Jonathan was true to his word of not keeping Luca's secret. First, he told Madison, who told her best friend, Shanda, who told Trevor, who told Monique, who told Mikaela, who told, well, everyone who had a working set of ears. By the last period of the day, the air was filled with snickering. Luca knew why. Within three hours, he had gone from a popular kid with numerous friends to being the kid everyone laughed at. He wanted to strangle those talking cats.

Mr. Bursley was a no-nonsense teacher, and he wanted to quell the snickering immediately. "Would someone like to tell me what's so darn funny?"

There was immediate silence. And then—

"Luca thinks his cats talk," said Jonathan, who was sitting parallel to Luca.

The whole class erupted into laughter.

"Shut up, Jonathan!" yelled Luca.

"Why don't you make me?" replied Jonathan.

And before he knew it, Luca launched himself toward the boy who had been his best bud for five years, and the two of them rolled on the ground, neither landing a punch, before Mr. Bursley broke them up and dragged them to the principal's office, a place neither had ever visited, with the exception of relaying a message or an envelope from a teacher.

"What on Earth has gotten into you two?" asked Principal Strickland.

They sat in silence.

"One of you needs to start talking."

"Luca told me that his cats talk. Not just meowing, but actual words."

"Is this true, Luca?"

"I told him not to tell anyone, and then he blabbed it to everyone. And now I'm getting made fun of."

"You two have always been good boys, so I'm going to let you return to Mr. Bursley's class on one condition: no more nonsense, no angry words, and certainly no fighting."

They both thanked their principal and got up to return to class.

"But I will have to call your parents," she said.

This bit of news elicited groans from both boys, but she hushed them with a gentle raise of her hand. "They need to be aware of what's going on here, young men. Now, back to class for the both of you."

The two boys walked back to class in silence, which was broken only by the subtle meowing Luca was greeted with upon entering the room.

"One more meow out of any of you, and I'll see to it that you're suspended for three days. Do I make myself clear?" said Mr. Bursley.

There was no meowing for the rest of the day, and while Luca was glad to be leaving school, he needed to have a serious conversation with the sources of his troubles.

"Hello?" said Vic.

"Mr. Gioppolo? This is Principal Strickland. I'd like to have a word with you about Luca."

The principal's tone made Vic's heart skip a beat.

"I hope it's nothing serious."

"Well, it's just that he and Jonathan got into a bit of a scrape. Is it possible to see you and your wife in person? It might be easier to explain."

"Well, Claudia doesn't get home till after 5:00. Maybe first thing tomorrow morning?"

"Yes, that will work."

"I hope it's just boys being boys. I remember when I was 11—"

"It's a bit more complex than that, I'm afraid. I'd rather have this conversation in person."

"Of course. We'll see you in the morning."

Vic immediately called Claudia.

"Bad time?"

"No, just out of a meeting. What's up?"

"Luca's principal wants to see us. He and Jonathan apparently got into a fight."

"Yeah, it happens. They're 11-year-old boys."

"That was my first thought, too, but she's indicating it's more serious than just roughhousing preteens. The thing is, he'll be home any minute. Should I press him for details?"

"Why don't we hear what she has to say first and then confront him?"

"Yeah, I agree. See you in a couple hours."

And as Vic was hanging up the phone, in walked Luca.

"Hey, pal. How was your return to school?"

"It was fine. Why are you asking?"

Vic chuckled. "Because every day for the past six years, I've asked how your day was the second you walked through the door. Would you like me to stop?"

Luca noticed that his father was acting completely normal. Maybe Principal Strickland was bluffing. Maybe she wasn't going to call. Maybe this whole thing would blow over in a few days, and eventually he'd be able to laugh it off as a joke.

"No, Dad, school was fine. I just have a lot of makeup homework."

"All right, well, don't let me stop you. I have to get back to work, too."

And as soon as Vic was safely ensconced in his office, Luca called a meeting with the cats.

"You guys got me in trouble at school today."

He proceeded to tell them the entire ordeal, and while they felt bad, Red spoke for both of them when he said, "Luca, we told you not to tell anyone."

"But Jonathan is—was my best friend."

"Dude, no one's going to believe you, not even your parents. Think about it. You know it's true because you caught us in the act. Would you believe it if Jonathan told you he had talking cats?" asked Red.

"No. But he's my friend. I wouldn't go telling everyone about it to make him look bad."

"Maybe it'll blow over, Luca," said Fatty. "I'm sure something else will happen that catches everyone's attention, and by the end of the week, no one will even remember."

Luca hoped Fatty was right. Through dinner, everything appeared to be normal. Neither his mom nor dad let on that anything was amiss, that the principal had called, that he was in trouble. He went to bed that night exhausted from the day's events but hopeful that soon enough it would all pass over, like a brutal but quick summer storm.

"Mr. and Mrs. Gioppolo, your son has always been an excellent student, and we've never had a bit of trouble from him. So, this is somewhat difficult to say, I'm afraid," said Principal Strickland.

Claudia and Vic exchanged quick glances.

"It seems the reason Luca and Jonathan engaged in fisticuffs yesterday was because during recess, Luca informed Jonathan that his cats talked to him."

Claudia and Vic both chuckled.

"Our cats talk to him? You mean, like, in English?" asked Claudia.

"Yes. He told Jonathan in confidence, but Jonathan proceeded to tell other students, and, before you know it, the whole class is making fun of Luca. Luca is an only child, correct?"

"Yes," said Claudia.

"Does he have—"

"Imaginary friends?" said Vic, seeing where the conversation was heading. "A whole team of them when he was younger. I figured he had outgrown that stage."

"Well, could it be that he's imagined that the cats are talking to him? I've looked at his school records. He's a creative child. And we have school psychologists who can—"

"Whoa. Let's take it one step at a time," said Claudia. "We'll talk to our son and get to the bottom of this. Let's not jump to conclusions."

"Of course not, Mrs. Gioppolo. I assure you we all want what's best for young Luca. But please talk to him."

"Thank you, Principal Strickland, for bringing this to our attention," said Vic. "We will keep you updated."

Luca went the entire day without being mocked. But, in a way, what was happening now was even worse: He was being shunned. He was invisible, even to Jonathan, who didn't make eye contact with him once.

Luca's conversation with his father upon arriving home was routine. Luca was now convinced that his principal had been bluffing.

Until dinner.

"So, buddy, we'd like to hear in your words happened with Jonathan at school yesterday," said Vic.

And Luca had been enjoying his mac-n-cheese so much.

"I don't want to talk about it."

"That's not an option," said Claudia. She had her serious-mom look on. Luca knew he had to come clean.

"I told him a story, and he didn't believe me. And he told everyone about it. And they were making fun of me. So, I attacked Jonathan."

"Back up, pal," said Vic. "What was this story about?"

"I told him . . . something about the cats."

Four eyes were boring into him.

"I told him the cats talked to me."

"Luca, it's wonderful to be imaginative. But there's a difference between that and lying," said Vic.

"But I'm not lying!"

"Honey, our cats meow, and Red can be pretty vocal, but they don't 'talk' talk," said Claudia.

"But they do!" And with that, he ran from the table, headed upstairs, and slammed his door shut.

Red and Fatty had been listening the whole time. They felt horrible for Luca, but they decided they couldn't bail him out. They just couldn't be sure how Claudia and Vic would react.

"You know, as a parent, you expect to face certain problems—maybe a broken bone playing sports, the occasional bad test grade—but talking cats? Where did that come from?" asked Vic.

"He's a creative boy. It's probably normal," said Claudia. "The thing that worries me most is his reputation at school. I don't want him to be the outcast."

As they were talking, in walked Red, being more vocal than usual.

"And there's our talking cat. Come on, Red. Do you have anything to add?" asked Vic.

"We need to think of something to salvage our son's reputation," said Claudia.

Red vocalized again, looking directly at Vic.

"You sure are one smart cat, Reddy Redson."

"What?" asked Claudia.

"Let me go talk to the boy. Red just gave me a really good idea."

Vic knocked lightly on Luca's bedroom door as he entered. "Hey, buddy, can we talk for a minute?"

"I'm not lying, Dad. And I'm not crazy. The cats talk."

Vic sighed.

"Remember when your pal Jonathan—"

"He's not my pal anymore."

"Okay, understood. Remember when Jonathan broke a couple fingers after he fell off his bike?"

"Yeah."

"Sometimes people break bones, right? And they go to a doctor, and they get them fixed. Well, sometimes people's brains need a doctor's attention. And that's totally normal and nothing to be afr—"

"I don't need to see any kind of doctor, Dad! Why won't you believe me?!"

"Because cats don't talk, honey!"

Vic could see he was upsetting Luca, and he didn't want to escalate the situation.

"Okay, champ. Let's focus on the immediate problem. Are you getting made fun of by your classmates?"

"No. They're just ignoring me now. I'm officially the weird kid. It sucks."

"Maybe Red could help you in your predicament."

"Dad, Red's part of the reason I'm in this predicament."

"Well, then, maybe he'll feel compelled to help you."

For the next two days, Vic made it his quest for Red to become a talking cat. After doing some research, he figured a snack reward would be the best approach.

"Hey, Reddy," he would say, holding a bag of treats. When Red would meow, Vic would give him a couple treats. But when he was silent, there was no treat. Red didn't seem to be getting the hang of it.

"Honey, I admire your dedication, but do you really think this will work?" asked Claudia.

"He's a smart cat. I've watched dozens of YouTube videos where this works. Just give me some time."

Red, of course, thought this was the funniest thing in the world.

"How long do you plan on dragging this out, Red?" asked Fatty.

"Fatty, don't you understand? It has to be convincing. Plus, I've been getting, like, a dozen extra snacks every day. Are you jealous?"

"That was a cheap shot. But you might want to speed things up. Luca's still getting the outcast treatment at school."

Finally, a week into Vic's experiment, he produced a remarkable breakthrough.

"Okay, Reddy, one meow for one snack."

"Meow."

"Okay, how about two meows for two snacks?"

"Meow-meow."

Vic was so excited, he called in Claudia and Luca.

"All right, Reddy, I'll give you three snacks for three meows."

"Meow-rowr-rowr!"

Claudia was as excited as Vic. Luca glared at Red.

"Honey, that's amazing! Your hard work paid off!"

"I knew we could do it. All right, Reddy, let me call Luca's teacher, and you can repeat your performance for his classmates."

When Luca and the cats were alone, Red offered his most heartfelt apology.

"Look, Luca. We know we're the reason you're being shunned by your friends. I promise you I'll put on a heck of a show for them. It's the least I can do."

"Thanks, Red. I never should have told Jonathan. It's not your or Fatty's fault. I just wish my parents believed me."

"Give it time, Luca," said Fatty. "Let's just take this first step of restoring your reputation in school."

Three days later, Mr. Bursley's science class featured a special guest.

"Boys and girls," Mr. Bursley said, "you are too old for show-and-tell, but special circumstances call for exceptions."

The kids were growing animated. They had no idea what was about to occur.

"Ladies and gentlemen, boys and girls of all ages, I present to you Luca and his talking cat, Red."

And in walked Luca, holding a bag of cat snacks and a stool, scared at what was about to transpire, and Red, who was basking in the attention. Red, of course, knew the performance would be 100 percent successful. There'd probably even be hoots for an encore, he reasoned.

Red hopped onto the stool.

"Okay, Red. You know how this goes—one meow for one snack."

"Meow."

"Good job, boy."

The class was unimpressed.

"Would you like two snacks, Reddy?"

Red kept silent. He liked building up the drama.

Then, finally, "Meow-meow."

A few kids started to chuckle. Red knew he was winning them over.

"Good job. But would someone like three snacks?"

Again, he said nothing immediately. He scanned the room. He spotted Jonathan and sensed his remorse for causing his friend so much grief.

"Meow-rowr-rowr!"

And with that bellowing meow, Red had won over the entire class, who erupted into a cheer.

"Very good, Luca—and Red," said Mr. Bursley. "So, you see, class, Luca does have a talking cat."

And that talking cat didn't want the show to be over just yet. So, quick as a sneeze, he leapt onto the middle of Mr. Bursley's desk, reached up like a meerkat and said, "Meow-rowr-rowr-meow!"

Luca gladly handed over four snacks to Red as the class continued applauding. Red was a hit, and Luca would be welcomed back by his friends.

But before Luca brought Red back to a waiting Vic, Red jumped on Jonathan's desk and gave him a good stare.

"Okay, Red, let's go," said Luca.

But Red wouldn't budge. He kept staring at the boy who had caused Luca anguish.

"I-I'm sorry, Luca," said Jonathan.

Satisfied, Red jumped off the desk, tail waving high as he departed the room, his performance a boffo success.

Vic could tell by the smile on Luca's face that Red had delivered.

"Well, if it isn't Luca and his amazing talking cat!"

"Red was great, Dad! He even jumped on Mr. Bursley's desk and meowed four times!"

"Reddy Redson, you slayed!" said Vic.

Red was tempted to say, "Again, Papa, it's Red. Simply Red. Red Flame on occasion, but enough with this 'Reddy Redson' business." But he didn't. He just basked in the glow of his stage debut.

Red hated the car ride home. He was bursting with energy, yet he was stuck in the carrier. As soon as they reached the house, he flew out of the carrier and circumnavigated the first floor several times.

Vic laughed, congratulated Red once more on his performance, and headed back to his office.

As soon as the coast was clear, Red gave Fatty his biased review.

"You should have seen me, Fatty! I killed!"

"Is Luca back in with his friends?"

"Yep. And get this. I gave his pal Jonathan a good talking-to."

"You did what?!"

"With my eyes, friend. But he got the message. And I even jumped on the teacher's desk and gave everyone a four-meow encore. They loved it."

"Good job, Red, and that buys us some time to figure out what to do."

"What are we doing?"

"Red, all this did was restore Luca's reputation with his friends. And yes, that's important, but our parents still think there's something wrong with Luca or that he's a liar."

"You worry too much, Fatty. Just let nature take its course. They'll find out the truth when they're meant to."

"Or they'll find it out at the worst time imaginable."

"Oh, hush. You're just cranky because I got all those sweet bonus snacks today, not to mention the fawning praise of an entire classroom and the teacher."

"You were full of yourself before today. I'm not sure I can cope with the new-and-inflated Red."

"Do you have a choice, Fatty dear?"

Fatty sighed and decided it was a good time for a nap.

"Hey, Dad. Happy Father's Day."

It was almost 8:00 at night. The old man wondered if they had drawn straws to see who would call first.

"Thanks, Martin. How're Beth and the kids?"

"They're good, Dad. Michaela's graduating high school this year, if you can believe it."

"I can't. Time flies, huh?"

They exchanged banalities for a few more minutes, with the old man thinking the whole time, "It's only a 20-minute trip. Would it kill you to visit?"

He thanked his son once again for the card and 5-pound bag of barbecued almonds, and that was that.

Within the hour, he and his daughters performed the same routine—MaryBeth's the ace pitcher of her school softball team, Bella starts student-teaching next semester, and yes, thank you for the fishing lures—and the painful exercise was finally over.

And he was alone, which he hated. But it beat the heck out of stilted phone conversations with his children. He knew for them it was nothing more than a chore—walk the dog, take out the trash, and oh, yeah, it's Father's Day. Let's call the old drunk and get this over with.

He envisioned them calling each other afterward and comparing notes. The spouses and grandkids probably got in on the act, too.

And what was worse was that he knew he had only himself to blame for their behavior. He drove them away. And why would they want to spend time with him and subject their children to such a visit? He barely could stand being with himself.

So, he'd spend the rest of Father's Day eating almonds and washing them down with whatever he had in the house while watching the Pirates struggle in the sixth year of their newest five-year rebuilding plan.

His only companions were his memories, and he could never figure out which were worse: the good ones, which broke his heart, or the bad ones, which shattered it.

The Buccos were losing 8–1 in the seventh inning. Sleep couldn't come fast enough for Franklin. With any luck, he thought, he wouldn't bother waking up.

"Did you pick out this tie by yourself, Luca?"

"Well, Mom helped, but I know you like blue."

"I do, pal, except when I think it's purple. Thanks. Oh, and what do we have here? Is this the pound box of Sarris chocolate-covered pretzels? I might need some help with this one, guys."

"Not a problem, dear. Happy Father's Day."

"Thanks, Claud."

School had ended a week earlier, and while Luca's friends had largely forgotten about the talking-cat incident, Vic and Claudia were still concerned about their son's well-being, unsure if he was just being overly imaginative or someone prone to telling tall tales.

But the subject had largely been forgotten, and they would have all summer to monitor their son's behavior.

"Oh, wait, honey. There is one more present—from the cats."

"The cats got me a gift? That's so sweet of them."

Upon hearing this, Red and Fatty walked into the living room, curious to see what they had bought Vic.

"Oh, speak of the devils," said Vic, opening their gift. "Three box seats to next week's Pirates game? Red and Fatty, you shouldn't have! Thanks, guys."

Vic gave hugs and kisses all around, and the family made its way into the dining room for dinner.

"That's not what I would have bought Papa," said Red.

"What would you have gone with?" asked Fatty.

"Catnip seeds."

"A Father's Day present is supposed to be for him, not for us, Red."

"Okay, sure, ultimately, it would be for us, but the planting and watering and maintenance would be a family project. See? Everybody wins."

"Gifts aren't supposed to be selfish."

"Whatever, Fatty. Our gift is a good one. If they're at the baseball game, that means we have the house to ourselves. We can do whatever we want."

"What should we do? Open up the door and let all the strays in and have a wild party?"

"No, but I do have something in mind, friend."

"Why do I not like the sound of what you're saying, Red?"

"Because you like being nervous, Fatty. Just relax and hear me out. You ready?"

"Do I have a choice?"

"Nope. Good point, Fatty. Anyway, here goes. We pay a visit to your old friend."

"Who's my old friend, Red?"

"You know, the infamous 'two-legged.'"

"What?! Why would I want to do that? Besides, how do you propose we get out of here, even if I agreed to your crazy idea?"

"That's easy. We like to look out of Luca's bedroom window, right? Well, we'll just make sure one of us is sitting there when they go to the game. A little lift of the screen, a hop onto the porch roof, another hop onto the grass, and boom, we're free."

"There's so much wrong with that idea, Red, I'm not sure where to start."

"It's a beautiful plan, my portly chum."

"Okay, for starters, how do we lift the screen?"

"Between our four paws—okay, three functional paws—I have no doubt we can nudge it enough to escape."

"Perhaps. But you're forgetting something. I can jump down, but jumping back up isn't for me."

"Hmm, you're right, Fatty. I had forgotten you're more earthbound than I am."

Red was dismayed that there was such a hole in his plan.

"Well, I'll think of something. Don't worry."

"I'm not worried, Red, because it's not going to happen. Similarly, I don't worry about shark attacks or elephant stampedes."

"You're being dismissive and hurtful."

"I'm being realistic, Red."

"Can you honestly tell me you don't want to feel the grass under your paws again, Fatty? And aren't you just a little curious to see how the human who hurt you is doing?"

Fatty stared at Red, and her gaze lingered a beat too long.

"Ah! I knew it!"

"But your scheme has serious flaws, Red. If we do this—and that's a huge 'if'—we do it on my terms."

"Agreed."

"First, we need to talk to Luca."

Luca was in his room, strumming his guitar. Red jumped onto his bed.

"What do you guys want?"

"Luca, did I ever tell you the story of how my leg got bent?"

Luca felt bad for his friend upon hearing her sad tale and gave her a loving head pat before asking, "That's horrible, Fatty, but why are you telling me this now?"

"Because we want to pay the jerk a visit."

"Red, hush. I miss being outside. I just want to take a walk, feel the grass under my paws, and maybe—maybe—stroll by the mean man's house, just out of curiosity."

"But I can't let you guys out. You could get hurt. I'd get in huge trouble."

"All you have to do is leave your window and screen open a crack the night you guys go to the baseball game. Then, when you return home, let me in the back door, since I can't jump."

"No! You guys almost ruined my entire year at school, and Mom and Dad won't bring up the issue because they're afraid that I still think you guys talk, and they're right, because you do!"

Red started to speak but was hushed quickly by Fatty. "Listen, Luca. I understand. You know our secret, and we've given you a terrible burden. But I miss being outside sometimes. Don't get me wrong. Kind Sir and Mom and you saved my life and have given me a wonderful home. It's just, well, I am an animal, after all. We won't stay out more than 20 minutes. I promise."

She and Red both gave Luca their best sad-eyed stares.

"Okay, fine! You get 20 minutes. Run through the grass or whatever it is you want to do and get back on the porch."

"Thanks, Luca!" they said in unison and happily let Luca return to his guitar.

"You're a smooth talker, Fatty. Nice work."

"Don't thank me yet. A lot of things can go wrong."

"Nonsense! Next Saturday night will be awesome."

"What if the game goes to extra innings, and I'm stuck on the porch for hours and—"

"Stop worrying, friend. Draw up an itinerary for our trip if it'll calm your nerves."

"Don't you ever worry, Red?"

"Of course, Fatty. I worry when my food bowl gets low. I worry when someone grabs the vacuum cleaner, because that sound is the worst. And I worry that my friend worries too much."

Fatty gave Red a head-butt as a way of saying thanks and then headed to the kitchen to see the status of the food bowls. To her relief, they were almost full.

THE BASEBALL GODS DELIVERED the following Saturday. Game-time temperatures were in the upper 60s, and there was hardly a cloud in the sky. PNC Park would shine like the jewel it is, with its backdrop of the picturesque downtown Pittsburgh skyline echoing the cheers of 35,000 fans, among them being the Gioppolo family, completely unaware that 15 miles away, two curious cats were about to embark on a much quieter adventure of their own.

As promised, Luca left his window and screen open just enough for them to launch on their journey.

They each got onto the windowsill and jumped onto the porch roof two feet below. The jump from the porch roof onto the grass, however, was a bit more daunting, but they both handled it well, the only difference being that Red stuck his landing, unlike Fatty, who rolled to a stop upon landing in the backyard grass. What she lacked in grace, she made up for in determination.

"Now, listen, Red. You haven't been outside since you were rescued as a kitten. If you think you can't handle—"

"I can handle myself perfectly well outdoors, Fatty. What makes you think I can't—ah! What's that?"

"It's a grasshopper, tough guy. He's about as harmless as—well, he's about as harmless as you are."

"Pfft! I can be plenty harmful, Fatty."

"Yeah, you're right, Red. Why, just the other day, you shoved one of Mom's spider plants to the floor. He was a ferocious foe, huh?"

"Oh, I didn't mean to shove it. I just took a nibble, and, well, gravity took over. But it did make a cool sound."

"Yeah, and it was cool the way the dirt splattered all over the floor, too, right?"

"I felt bad that Mama had to clean it up. What was I supposed to do, apologize?"

"Maybe just be more careful, Red?"

"Fine. Let's just stay focused, Fatty. Hello, Mr. Grasshopper!"

"He doesn't talk, Red."

"Did you ever encounter any other animal who did, Fatty?"

"Nope. You're the first and only, Red."

The cats walked through the backyard grass, taking turns rolling around before reaching the fence, which they quickly climbed. They were now in the neighbor's yard, where they playfully waved at their neighbor dog, who was looking out the window. He didn't wave back.

From backyard to backyard they went, rolling in the grass, chasing fireflies, waving at various pets in windows, even being so bold as to jump on a windowsill and tap hello at a calico, who quickly scurried away, which Red and Fatty thought was hysterical.

"Wasn't this a great idea, Fatty?"

"I have to admit it. It was. But if you want to see where the two-legged lives, you're going to have to cross a street."

"Just lead the way, friend."

They reached the end of their street, but since it was almost 10:00, there was no traffic. Crossing was easy, and they resumed their backyard tour, saying hello to insects and pets and having a grand time until Fatty suddenly got serious.

"That's the window well, Red. This is the house."

Red immediately jumped on the living-room windowsill.

"Red, don't!"

"No, it's okay, Fatty. Your pal is asleep in a recliner. There's an empty bottle at his feet. He's watching Pirate highlights. That means the game's over. See, Fatty? No extra innings. And, hey, they won. Luca will be happy."

Fatty joined him on the sill. She felt bad for the man who had hurt her. She looked around his living room. It was a mess, with newspapers and magazines scattered around. The burned-out lightbulbs outnumbered the functioning ones. The main glow came from the old television. There were dirty bowls on the table and utensils on the floor. If a museum were attempting to capture gloom and despair, they would pack up the entire room and re-create it in their space.

"I noticed there's a hole in the window, Fatty. Apparently, his fix was temporary. We could pop in and say hello."

"No, Red. I've seen enough for now. Let's head back. We don't want to worry Luca."

And so they hopped down and retraced their steps back to their home. They playfully gave chase to a few more insects, waved at as many pets as they saw, took one long roll in their own backyard, and were glad to see the family car in the driveway.

Red quickly hopped back onto the porch roof. "All right, Fatty. I'm going to shoot back into Luca's room and tell him you need to be let in. Give me a second."

And boom, he was gone. Fatty admired her friend's athleticism.

"Luca, there's a chubby feline waiting for you to let her in. Hurry."

As she was giving the yard a loving stare, she noticed a furtive Luca approaching the door.

"Quick, get in."

And the adventure was over. Luca wouldn't get in trouble, and Claudia and Vic were none the wiser.

"See, Fatty? You worried for nothing," said Red. "When's our next outing?"

"Uh . . . never?"

"Fatty, tell me you didn't love it."

"I did love it, Red. But let's not press our luck. It was fun. Enjoy that it happened."

Red was too tired to keep up the argument. He knew that it wouldn't take much to sell Fatty on a sequel, but the adventure had worn them both out, and soon they shut their eyes, chasing grasshoppers in their sleep.

THEY AWOKE ITCHY.

"Fatty, what's going on? This is horrible."

"I think we have fleas, Red. We took home a souvenir from our trip."

"I knew we should have opted for the T-shirt or coffee mug, pal. Now what?"

"Well, our people will see us itching, and they'll take us to the vet."

It didn't take long for Vic and Claudia to know something was amiss, as they were itching almost as much as the cats.

"Honey, my white sock is quite the gathering place for our new friends. How could this have happened? The cats never leave the house."

"Well, all it takes is a couple fleas to sneak in. Remember how nice the weather was last week? We had the windows open. I guess I'll call the vet."

"Yeah, what choice do we have, Claud?"

In walked Luca.

"Mom, Dad, my ankles are itchy and bit up. Do you think mosquitoes got us at the game?"

"No, buddy. I think our feline friends somehow attracted a following of fleas. We'll have to take them to the vet and get it cleared up."

Instantly, Luca felt bad that he had green-lighted the cats' adventure. First, they made him a temporary school outcast, and now the whole family was itchy because of their escapade.

He traipsed back to his room, with the cats following.

"Luca, we're sorry, but if it's any consolation, we're the ones who have to go to the vet. The carrier, the car ride, whatever medicine they give us—it's all horrible. But the worst part? The vet has cold hands," said Fatty.

"It's true, Luca. And it's not like we can tell her," said Red. "We have to be in full-cat mode the whole time. But we are sorry, pal."

"If Mom and Dad find out I let you out, I'd probably be grounded till I'm 18."

"We won't tell if you won't, Luca," said Red.

Luca sighed and shooed the cats from his room.

THEIR PORTABLE KITTY PRISONS were sitting by the door. Fatty instinctively put her good paw on the outside of the cage, but she knew resistance was futile, and she didn't want to make it needlessly harder for Vic.

Karma worked quickly. She and Red were being punished for their sneaky adventure, and now they had to go to the vet's and endure the pain of being regular cats for however long the trip and visit lasted. Mum was the word.

"All right, knuckleheads, let's get going," said Vic as he loaded the two escapees into the backseat. He situated himself, buckled up, and as soon as he flipped on the radio, the cats knew they were in for an impromptu concert featuring a horrible singer. And unlike in the house, where they could quickly scamper away whenever Vic displayed his complete lack of vocal abilities, this time, there was no escape.

Red and Fatty both had the same thought, though they were unable to communicate with each other. They couldn't decide what was worse: his off-key singing or the fact that he made up most of the words. Mercifully, the radio station went to a commercial break.

"What's so bad about the vet's office, guys?"

"The vet has cold hands, Kind Sir."

Vic momentarily lost control of the steering wheel and had to pull over.

"Did you just talk, Fatty?"

"Marowr."

Vic took a quick inventory of his existence. He was a sane man, a father, a husband. He worked in public relations. He was a stable, taxpaying citizen. His idea of a wild time was having a second beer while watching a Penguins game.

"I'm going to ask you again. Did you just talk, Fatty?"

"Yes, Kind Sir."

65

"I'm guilty, too, Papa," Red said.

"'Papa,' 'Kind Sir.' What on Earth is going on?!"

"I call you 'Papa,' Papa. Fatty opts for 'Kind Sir.' I call your wife Mama and your son 'the boy.' Fatty, meanwhile, opts for 'Mom' and—and what do you call the boy?"

"I call him Luca, Red," said Fatty.

"Of course."

Vic tried to convince himself he was having a dream, but everything outside the car appeared to be completely normal. Cars were zipping by. The sun was shining. There were no giraffes galloping in the distance or pterodactyls flying above. Neither Abraham Lincoln nor Winston Churchill nor any other out-of-place historical figure was sitting in the passenger seat.

Vic slowly turned to face the cats and did his best to present a picture of serenity. His quivering hands betrayed him.

"We can explain, Papa, sort of. We talk. Fatty stumbled onto our backyard, and we instantly knew. We were fast friends, and I convinced her—eventually—that you guys were safe."

Vic still couldn't believe what he was seeing and hearing, but everything outside the car continued to remain normal—no unicorns, no army of George Washingtons juggling footballs while singing selections from "Cabaret." Everything was routine. A biker zipped by. A voice was blathering on the radio about the new casino in town.

"Luca," said Vic.

"Oh, yeah, Papa. You and Mama are going to have to give him a huge apology."

"Kind Sir, we need to apologize, too. It's just—"

"Fatty, there's a lot to sort out here. But first, we need to get to the vet's in time."

They drove the rest of the way in silence. The cats picked up on the vibe that Vic was clinging to sanity. He turned the radio on and off a half-dozen times, unsure if the radio would help ground him or send him to the point of no return if he heard the wrong word. Finally, they arrived at the vet's.

"Now listen, you two. I can't believe I have to say this, but for the duration of this visit, you are normal cats. I'm still trying to convince myself that this is all a weird dream or a temporary bout of insanity, but do you understand? No talking."

They both nodded in assent, which both pleased and bemused Vic. He took several deep breaths, trying to steady himself before entering the office. He was exceedingly normal, he told himself. He drives a Camry. His only vice is chocolate. He pays his bills on time. He's a generous tipper. Everything is fine. He will go into the office with two normal cats in tow. He will be pleasant to the receptionist and the various pets and owners who are there with him. He will get the cats their flea medication and pay for it at the reception desk. He will then return the cats to the car and drive his very normal car back to his very normal home, where he lives with his very normal son and wife. They will have a very normal dinner, and after dinner he may toss a baseball around with Luca in the backyard in a very normal way. Everything is fine.

"Hi. My name's Vic. I'm here for Red and Fatty's appointment." There. He passed the first test. The pleasant receptionist told him to have a seat and wait till he was called. The waiting area was filled with cats and dogs and their owners. There wasn't a platypus in sight, nor a great white shark playing the violin. Everything was as it should be. Vic sat patiently and exchanged smiles with the other pet owners, occasionally sneaking a peek into Red's and Fatty's carriers, prompting Red to stick out his tongue at Vic upon the third check-in. So, everything was as it should be, save for the fact that Vic and his family possessed talking cats, one of whom was a wise guy.

Finally, Vic's name was called, and as he brought the two carriers into the examination room, he peered into Red's one final time, only to see that Red had rolled his eyes back into his head and was flopping around, pretending to be dying. Vic cleared his throat, perhaps a bit too loudly, but Red got the hint and straightened up. Vic couldn't wait for this visit to be over, and he was hoping his showman cat could keep it together for a few more minutes.

"Mr. Gioppolo, it says here on the chart that you're the proud owner of two very itchy cats," said Dr. Amoroso.

Vic chuckled. "Yep, I'm not sure how it happened, but I guess they have fleas. That's pretty routine, right? You can just prescribe some medicine, and we'll be on our way."

"Well, I will need to examine them to make sure there isn't another cause. Are you in a hurry?"

"No, well, it's just, I see you have a whole arkful of animals out there. I wouldn't want to keep them waiting." Vic chuckled nervously.

The vet gave Vic an odd look. "Okay, well, let's see what we have here." She undid the latch to Fatty's carrier and let her free. Fatty grimaced, knowing what was coming. And as soon as the vet placed her hands on Fatty's neck, Fatty tensed up—as did Vic—but remained silent as she endured the vet's icy hands.

She then examined Red, who kept his antics to a minimum—a quick eye-cross for Vic's pleasure; he didn't find it amusing—before saying, "Yep, it's fleas. I'll prescribe an ointment that will start working almost instantly."

"Ah, that's good to hear, doc. So, how would indoor cats get fleas, anyway? These two never leave the house."

"All it takes is two fleas stowing away on the bottom of a shoe or sneaking in through a screen. It happens. But they'll be fine in no time. Goodbye, kitties," she said.

Vic held his breath and literally froze, fearing that one of them— probably Red—would feel compelled to respond.

"Is everything okay, Mr. Gioppolo?"

"Oh, um, you know how it is. I'm busy at work, and I had to get these two here, and now I'm going to have to play catch-up the rest of the day. But everything's fine. Thank you."

And Vic was finally able to leave the vet's office and could resume normal breathing patterns, his secret safe.

"Thank you for not talking, though, Red, I could have done without the faces."

"Red, what did you do?" asked Fatty.

"Well, first, I hit him with the stuck-out tongue. Then, I rolled my eyes back and played dead. Finally, the tried-and-true eye cross. But Papa kept his cool. Good job, Papa."

"Yeah, thanks, Red. Alternatively, you could have done, let's see, nothing. Yeah, nothing. That probably would have been the better option."

"Yeah, well, what's done is done. I'm entertaining. I can't simply turn off that switch. So, how are we telling Mama? And what are you two going to say to the boy?"

"Well, 'we' aren't telling Claudia anything. I'm going to break it to her. And I have no idea how, but I certainly don't need any assistance from the talking cats."

"Ooh, 'Papa and the Talking Cats.' I like the sound of that," said Red. "We could take this act on the road. I'd be famous."

"Ah, yes, Red—the adulation of the adoring crowds, the fan mail, the incessant request for selfies every time you stepped paw outside. You'd love all that, I'm guessing?"

"You know it, Papa."

"Red, you sleep at least 18 hours a day. I've seen you literally hop off your pillow in the spare bedroom, walk downstairs, and resume your nap on the couch. Maybe a life of being hounded by the paparazzi isn't quite for you."

They drove the rest of the way home in silence, with Vic's logic subduing Red. But Vic's mind was racing. He still wasn't convinced he wasn't having the longest, most vivid dream of his life. Claudia would either confirm the existence of the talking cats or wake him from his slumber or call the first psychologist she found in the phone book and gently encourage her loving husband to get the help he clearly needed.

The ride home was boringly normal. There were billboards and fast-food joints along the way. Ordinary birds were flitting between ordinary trees. A paperboy was delivering the afternoon daily.

Finally, they pulled into the driveway. Claudia was home from work.

"All right, you two, remember. I'll do the talking."

Vic, cat carriers in tow, took a deep breath and entered his home, knowing that nothing would ever be the same again.

"Hey, babe. How are 'Itchy and Scratchy'?" She gave Vic a quick kiss.

Vic pointed at the cats and then at the dining-room chair that Luca usually occupies. He couldn't, however, seem to form any words.

"What? Is it something more serious than fleas?"

Vic shook his head, desperately seeking the best way to tell his wife the startling news.

"Mama, what Papa's trying to say is that Fatty and I talk. Luca will no doubt be waiting for an apology, or, better yet, the newest PlayStation games."

"Dang it, Red!" Vic finally found his words.

Claudia instinctively moved away from the cats and with trembling hands grasped onto Vic.

"Honey, what—what is going on?"

"Okay, Claud, here's what happened. Fatty accidentally blurted out her critique of the vet's cold hands while we were in transit. I had to pull the car over. I thought I was having a dream or losing my mind. But now? Now it's become very real for me, unless we're having the same dream or have gone crazy together."

"As we were saying to Kind Sir in the car, Mom—"

"Wait. Who's 'Kind Sir'?"

"I am, honey." Vic batted his long eyelashes in Claudia's direction.

"Oh, you're kind, too, Mom. It's just that Kind Sir was the first person I met here, and I trusted his kind eyes. I'm sorry, Mom."

"Oh, sweetie, that's fine. Your voice fits you so well. You're adorable! But, Vic, this isn't real. It can't be."

"Well, honey, let's review. Luca told his friends the cats talk. And now we've both confirmed that what Luca is saying is true. Red and Fatty talk. Is Luca still at Jonathan's?"

"Yep. He texted me a bit ago and asked if he could stay for dinner. I said yes."

"Okay, good. That buys us some time."

"If you want, you could put me on the phone with the boy, and I could catch him up to speed," said Red.

"No, Red, really, you've done enough today already," said Vic.

"Hey, for what it's worth, it was ol' Fatty who made you almost lose control of the car, Papa."

"I am sorry about that, Kind Sir."

"Okay, both of you, no more apologies. We get it. But Claudia and I will figure out what to say to Luca, and we don't need any help. Do you understand, Red?"

"I can make no promises, Papa."

"Red, you do realize now that your secret's out, we will no longer dismiss your various transgressions as 'Oh, he's just a cat. He doesn't know any better. He didn't mean to shove that plant off the windowsill.' There will be repercussions now."

"The gig's up, Red," said Fatty.

"Ooh, kitty time-outs will now be a thing," said Claudia. "Or no snacks if you misbehave."

"But, Mama, I love snacky-time! Dang it, Fatty, why'd you have to complain about the vet's cold hands? You could have just sucked it up and kept quiet. We had a good thing going."

"Oh, stop it, Red. One of us was going to slip up sooner or later. Don't you feel better that they know?"

"Well, maybe, but I don't want time-outs and snack deprivation."

"Then be a good kitty boy," said Claudia. "It's simple, Red."

"I am a good kitty boy, Mama. I'm just active sometimes. And I like a good show."

"All right, you two. Luca will be home soon. Run along and entertain yourselves or take a nap and let the ointment do its job," said Vic. "We need to have a serious chat with the boy. And we don't need your assistance, as much as you'd like to give it."

The cats listened, and Vic and Claudia sat at the dining-room table, figuring out the best way to apologize to an 11-year-old.

LUCA KNEW SOMETHING WAS up the second he saw his parents' faces.

"Is everything okay with the cats? Is it something worse than fleas?"

"No, Luca, it is fleas, and the cats are fine. But we had an interesting conversation on the way to the vet's."

Luca wasn't sure how to interpret what his father just said. He said nothing.

"We owe you an apology, honey," said Claudia.

"You mean . . ."

"I asked them what was so bad about going to the vet's, and, shock of my life, Fatty blurted out something about the vet having cold hands. I had to pull the car over."

"I told you guys! See? I wasn't lying!"

"Luca, we thought you were just having a very active imagination. I mean, you have to see it from our side, too," said Claudia.

Feelings of relief and anger rushed through Luca's brain. He was happy that the burden of his secret was no longer his alone, but he was still mad at his parents for not believing him from the get-go.

The cats figured it was safe to join the family.

"I guess we don't have to whisper to you anymore, buddy," said Red.

"Wait a minute," said Vic as a thought popped into his head.

"The weeks I spent 'training' you to perform at Luca's school—you knew every word I was saying. You could have revealed yourself then. Why didn't you?"

"Well, Kind Sir, we discussed numerous times the best way to tell you and Mom our secret, but usually the scenarios ended up with you passing out and hitting your head on a piece of furniture."

"So, you waited until I was driving on a highway for the big reveal?"

Fatty bowed her head dejectedly.

"No, Fatty, I'm teasing! It's okay. No one got hurt, and now we all know."

"Besides, Papa, wasn't it a confidence booster for you? You turned a savagely handsome, out-of-control beast into a pliable trick cat capable of entertaining schoolchildren in a matter of weeks. You, sir, are a master of the animal kingdom! Have you ever considered chucking your 9-to-5 and becoming a lion tamer?"

"It can be a harsh world outside these doors, Red. Ask Fatty."

"It's true, Red. You wouldn't last a half-hour."

"Pfft! Besides, you would never put me outside. I was entertaining before you knew our secret. Now? I can add entirely new dimensions to my routine."

"Also, you're not 'savagely handsome,'" said Fatty.

"Mama, as the other lady in the house, tell Fatty how wrong she is."

"Well, Fatty, Red is kind of a handsome bloke, I must admit."

"Thank you, Mama."

"You two make an adorable pair," said Claudia, prompting the cats to stare at each other before going in opposite directions, leaving the humans at least temporarily alone.

"Listen, buddy," said Vic. "Our secret can't leave the house. I'm still trying to process everything that's happened today. I can't even imagine how upside down our lives would become if anyone knew the truth about Red and Fatty."

"Yeah, Dad. I remember what happened at school. I'm not looking for a repeat."

Luca scampered off to his room. Vic embraced Claudia.

"Now what?" asked Claudia.

AURORA HAD A GOOD life. Her humans were kind and attentive. She had good food to eat and windows to look out of and comfortable beds and pillows and couches to nap on. And she was forever grateful to her humans for plucking her out of that animal shelter.

And now that they had moved from their somewhat cramped apartment into their new home, there were even more windows to look out of and places to explore.

But she possessed a secret, a secret she knew she could never reveal to Lisa and Keith—that's what the other humans called them—for fear of how they would react.

So, her days were quiet and content. But . . .

But when Lisa and Keith went to work, and Aurora was alone, there was one thought that invariably popped into her head: the last day she saw her boy.

It was such a bittersweet moment. She was so happy to be leaving the shelter but so heartbroken when she heard the humans say they could take only one cat. Oh, why didn't Lisa and Keith buy a house first and then go cat shopping? That way, mother and son could have shared a happy life together.

She prayed and hoped that he was well, that some nice human plucked him from the shelter and had given him a good home. Was he eating right? Was he happy? Did he have nice windows to look out of and comfy beds to nap on? It was her sincerest wish.

But what if he was still stuck at the shelter, alone and sad? Or, worse, what if he was in a horrible home with sad people who weren't treating him properly?

Aurora would drive herself sick with worry, but she knew there was nothing she could do to allay her fears. She was happy for the good fortune she was enjoying, but she would give anything to know that her boy was safe and happy.

It was futile, she knew. She would never see her sweet boy again. She would never again put paw to face or see his graceful leaps. She would never again hear his voice and the funny things he used to say or be able to retell the jokes they used to share about their fellow shelter inhabitants.

She could do nothing but wish that his life turned out as well as hers had.

But what she wouldn't give to spend even one more hour with that orange-and-white ball of fur who owned her heart.

She occasionally thought about sneaking out, but what good would that do? Where would she start looking? And her humans would be frantic. She didn't want to cause them pain. They had been so good to her.

Her life was good; she knew that. But there was a hole in her heart, and she was resigned to the notion that it would never be filled.

"Now what?" was a good question. Vic didn't have much of an answer.

He and Claudia were the parents of a sweet, wonderful boy and two nice cats. They had a perfectly ordinary life. And that perfect ordinariness was shattered today, when the cats revealed that they knew how to talk, a secret they accidentally shared with Luca a little while back. So, now the entire family was on the same page, and the adults had no idea how to proceed.

Were Red and Fatty the world's only talking cats? It didn't seem possible, but Red and Fatty knew instantly when they met that they shared the same gift, which had never happened when the two of them, in their separate lives, had encounters with other cats, be it at the shelter or outside.

If a cat with a grumpy face could make millions for its owners, imagine what talking cats could do. The possibilities were endless: TV appearances, movies, merchandise, social media. But Vic and Claudia were fond of their perfectly ordinary life and the safe environment they had built for Luca.

"We have to keep this our secret," said Claudia. "Yes, the money would be outrageous and life-changing, but would it be worth it? We'd be crazy-famous. We'd never have a moment's peace. Luca wouldn't be safe. Lunatics would try to steal our cats."

"You're probably right, Claud. Plus, with me being unfairly handsome, women throwing themselves at me would become a routine part of our lives."

"'Unfairly' handsome?"

"Okay, maybe not unfairly handsome, but . . . fairly handsome?"

"Hmm . . . in the right light, when I've had one glass too many . . . perhaps."

Vic chuckled.

So, it was decided. Red and Fatty's gift would be the family secret, shared with no one, under any circumstances. The money would be nice but not worth the disruptions that would inevitably follow.

"Plus, what if Red and Fatty are merely the first dominoes? We share their secret with the world. Then, before we know it, a huge army of talking cats reveals itself. They're smart and fast, and, boom, all of humanity is enslaved by cats."

"And Red is their leader," said Claudia.

"Wow. He'd probably treat us well, though, right? I mean, we've always been nice to him."

"True. And Fatty would never let anything bad happen to 'Kind Sir,' right?"

"Of course not, Claudia. Unless it's all a ruse. We think she's sweet, but, in reality, she's a monster watching our every step, waiting for us to make the wrong move."

"She has three functioning legs and can barely jump on the couch. I think we're safe."

"Ah, that's what they want us to think. They're laying their trap perfectly. This morning, we thought Luca's imagination got the best of him. Now we know he was telling the truth. Who knows what tomorrow will bring? Nothing makes sense anymore, Claudia! Humanity is on the verge of serfdom, and we're playing right into the enemies' hands! History will not speak well of us."

They both laughed, happy with their anonymous lives and fully content to not play a major role in the fall of humanity.

"Ah, I see she's brought a friend this time."

Franklin may have been in his usual drunken stupor, almost passed out in front of the television, but he was awake enough to see two cats peering in at him. And he recognized Fatty instantly and winced at the memory of how he had treated her in their previous interactions.

Part of him hoped they would sneak into his basement. It would give him a chance to show the kindness that he knew he possessed. But part of him also knew he was rarely his old self, having been replaced and fully consumed by the current version of Franklin Betters—drunk, angry, prone to fits of violence, and wallowing in sadness.

It was probably best that they scurried away. "At least she's found a friend. That's more than I can say. Maybe that's more than I deserve," he thought.

Even the Pirates winning on a starlit Saturday night did little to change his demeanor. The last he heard from his kids—or from anyone—had been on Father's Day. Three platitude-filled conversations and then back to Dylan's next ballgame or getting Michaela ready for college or whatever else filled their busy lives. Maybe one of the kids would call him before the Fourth of July and invite him for a picnic. And maybe he would say yes. He knew the invitations were halfhearted and that when he said no, he could feel the sense of relief on the other end of the line. He could almost hear them say to the others, "Well, what are you gonna do? We invited the old man, but he said no." He could see the other two nodding in assent, all feeling virtuous for having reached out, knowing full well that they were secretly relieved they wouldn't have to deal with him or make excuses for how he behaved in front of the kids.

But sometimes he said yes, because he wanted to see his kids and grandkids and be a part of their lives. He wanted it to be like the old times. It never was. He would have a belt or two before being picked up, just to calm his nerves, he'd tell himself. Then he'd have a beer when he arrived, you know, just to be social. Then he'd sneak another shot here and there, when he thought no one was watching. And, before long, he'd turn into the sad drunk, stumbling around, putting on a show for the grandkids. Then he'd be whisked away and deposited back to his house, with the wordless trip home being the worst part of the experience.

What could he say? How could he begin to apologize? He couldn't. So, he'd sit there in silence, feeling his child's disappointment fill the void.

"I was a good father, Martin," said Franklin on their way home from Christmas night last year.

"That, you were, Dad."

Martin didn't elaborate. The past-tense nature of their brief exchange made Franklin feel like he was a ghost.

The short yet mentally exhausting trip was finally over. Martin helped his father out of the car, unlocked the door, put on some lights, and admonished him to go directly to bed.

"How about I do whatever I want, son?"

"Fine. Have some more drinks. Stumble around, crack open your skull, if that's what you want. Fire up the Buick and terrorize the neighborhood while you're at it."

Martin felt bad as soon as the words escaped his lips. He sighed.

"Dad—"

"Stop, Martin. Go home, be with your family. Have a laugh at my expense."

"We don't laugh at you, Dad. We're just frustrated. This has been going on for years, and it's getting worse. Get help."

"Don't tell me what to do."

"Fine. Then, like I said—"

Martin stopped. He didn't want to escalate the situation.

"Just promise me you'll go to bed. Can I help you with anything?"

"No, and I will. Good night, son."

"Good night, Dad."

Martin was alone with his thoughts on the way home. It was Christmas night. There were few other cars on the road. After their mother unexpectedly died years ago, Martin and his sisters dismissed their father's drinking as a natural reaction. He was heartbroken, as they all were. So, they let it pass for fear of making it worse. Plus, how do you confront a parent when he or she has a problem? They've spent their entire lives guiding you, and now you're the one forced to admonish them? It's a difficult fit for most people.

But now? The situation was out of control. The kids and grandkids had come to expect Franklin's antics whenever they got together. It had become an unfortunate holiday tradition. Thanksgiving? Turkey, football, and drunken Grandpa. Easter? Ham, candy-filled baskets, and drunken Grandpa.

None of the grandkids knew a different Franklin, and that's perhaps what hurt Martin and his sisters the most. And they also knew that avoiding their father and his problem was worsening the situation.

Martin pulled into the driveway of his happy home, decorated perfectly for the season. He knew everyone was still there, and they would resume their festive time, breathing a collective sigh of relief that the old drunk was safely tucked away back in his dingy domicile.

Martin put on his happy face—his guests had endured enough—but his heart was in pain. He had to do right by his father. He wanted his children and Beth and his nieces to see the man he used to know and admire.

"So, that's why you hesitated coming into the house," said Vic to Fatty, after she explained to her humans what happened to her leg.

"Yep. She kept referring to you guys as the 'two-leggeds.' She thought you were all monsters," said Red. "I did my best to convince her otherwise."

"Aw, you poor thing," said Claudia. "Well, I'm glad you listened to Red."

"Just don't make that a habit," said Vic.

"Cheap shot, Papa," said Red.

"So, you say the house is a few blocks over, with a big front yard and a basketball hoop in the driveway that hasn't been used in forever?"

"Oh, that's Mr. Betters, isn't it?" said Claudia.

"You know the mean two-legged, Mom?"

"Well, kinda, Fatty. I mean, we don't know him that well. He wouldn't know our names, but . . ."

"But we know his story, Fatty. It's a sad one. It would explain a lot."

"He threw a candleholder at my friend and broke her leg. He's a mean, old drunk, and whatever sob story you're about to tell us doesn't justify his actions. I want to claw his face," said Red.

"No, Red, throwing things at animals isn't justified, but hear us out," said Vic. "And there will be no face clawings, either, it goes without saying."

"Franklin and his wife had three children—two girls and a boy," said Claudia. "They were the model of a happy family. They could have posed for the insert you see when you buy a picture frame—nothing but smiles and sunshine."

"Uh-oh. When stories start out like this, they always take a bad turn. Don't drag it out, Mama."

"Well," said Vic, "when their youngest, Jane, graduated from college and left home, Franklin and his wife—her name was Ruth—found themselves with a lot of time on their hands. Plus, they had done well in their professional lives. So, they decided to retire and see the world."

"And here comes the sad part. I don't like this story," said Red.

Claudia continued.

"Well, on the morning they were set to embark on their two-month European vacation, Ruth didn't wake up. She had a heart attack and passed in her sleep."

Red gasped.

"Franklin, of course, was devastated," said Vic. "He went to sleep dreaming of seeing the world with the love of his life, and he woke up a lonely man, with no wife and three adult children who had their own lives."

"That poor man," said Fatty.

"Who broke your leg," said Red.

"Be nice, Red. It doesn't justify what he did to me. But it does explain it."

"Anyway," said Claudia, "it was a slow spiral downward from that point on. He started drinking to numb the pain, and now he's a sad, old drunk shunned by all."

"There's a lesson here for all of us," said Vic. "Appreciate what you have in the moment. You never know when it's going to disappear."

"And the old man needs to be taught a lesson," said Red.

"Red, I'm the one who hobbles around because of him, and now that I've heard his story, well, yes, I'm still angry, but I feel horrible for him, too."

"You're a better cat than I am, Fatty."

"You really think so, Red?"

"No, Fatty. Don't be ridiculous."

"Okay, you two. It's dinnertime. And since you can now tell us what you want, instead of us guessing, what would you like?" said Vic.

"Hmm . . . I'm thinking turkey," said Red.

"Works for me," said Fatty. "I'm not a finicky cat."

"Luca," said Vic, "the cats have opted for a turkey can this evening, if you wouldn't mind."

"Sure, Dad."

"And a nice glass of Chardonnay, too, Luca," said Red.

Vic and Claudia looked at Red.

"What? In human years, I'm an adult. Break open the adult beverages, folks."

"I think you and your dining companion will be good with water and the occasional dollop of cream or milk," said Vic.

"Meh," said Red. "It was worth a shot."

The two cats followed Luca into the kitchen to enjoy their alcohol-free meal.

"We just had a lengthy conversation with two cats, Claud."

"Yeah, it's odd. What's even odder is that it's starting to seem normal."

"If we revealed them to the world, we'd be insanely rich."

"You're not serious, Vic."

"No, but imagine tooling around town in our Minion-yellow Jaguar."

"Do they even make yellow Jaguars?"

"Probably not, but we'd be so rich, we could call Mr. Jaguar himself and have it custom-made."

"So, the company was named after a man named Jaguar, you think?"

"Of course, Claud! Alessandro Jaguar. It's common knowledge. You really should crack open a book once in a while."

Claudia sighed. "With 'facts' like that in your head, I suppose it's a good thing you're unfairly handsome."

"Ah, I knew it! Hey, wait a second."

"What's on your mind, Reddy?" asked Vic.

Vic and Claudia and the cats were sitting in the living room, listening to Luca finish up his guitar lesson.

"How did you know something was on my mind?"

"Your tail's twitching, and your eyes keep darting back and forth. Unless you're about to pounce on a spider, I assume there's something going on in your brain."

"It's that story you guys told us before, about the two-legged."

"What about it, Red?" asked Claudia.

"It made me sad."

"It's a sad story, Red," said Fatty.

"Yes, but it made me sad in a particular way. It made me think of my mom."

Red told Claudia and Vic about the sad farewell he had with his mom at the shelter.

"She left months before I did, and, of course, that was it. I never saw her again. She could be anywhere. I miss her every day."

"Aw, honey, I had no idea," said Claudia.

Red head-butted Claudia as he departed, needing some alone time.

"He talks about her all the time," said Fatty. "I wish there were something we could do."

"Well," said Claudia, "they lived at the same shelter. And shelters must keep records, right?"

"True, but what's the approach? It's not like we can go there and say, 'Hi. We adopted an orange-and-white tabby from this place a while back. Turns out he had a mom who lived here, too. He told us how much he misses her, and we were wondering if you could give us any information on who took her so the two of them could have a reunion.'"

"Vic, honey, by profession, you create branding campaigns for companies so that people will buy things that those companies make. Surely you can do the same for Red."

"Well, probably, but how's Red going to afford me?"

"Do snuggles and purrs count as currency, Kind Sir?"

Vic gave Fatty a pat on her head. "More than you know, pal."

He realized that there was no need for a campaign, just the plain truth—minus, of course, any mention of Red and Fatty's unique gift.

"We'll try to swing by the shelter this weekend, Fatty, and give it a go. But don't mention anything to Red. We don't want to get his hopes up."

So, Claudia and Vic found themselves at the shelter the following Saturday morning. They saw the same hopeful faces on the cats, and they saw couples and families deciding which cats were going to get forever homes. They also tried, unsuccessfully, to figure out if any of the cats shared Red and Fatty's gift.

"Hi," said the volunteer who helped them with Red. "I remember you guys. How's our little Orville doing? Does he need a friend?"

"Oh, hello. Well, he's doing great, and, actually, we took in a stray not too long after we brought Orville home," said Claudia.

"But the thing is," said Vic, "is that he seems a little down sometimes, and we can't figure out what is causing it. Is it possible he had a special friend here or maybe a sibling or parent?"

"Well, yes, he was brought to the shelter with his mother, I believe. Hold on one second and let me check the records."

Vic and Claudia spent the next few minutes still trying to figure out if any of the cats talked, even going as far as to try to initiate conversations.

"Hello, young cat," said Vic to an approaching white longhair. The cat walked on by, aloof to Vic's attempted engagement.

"I think they're all just cats, Vic. You know, the regular variety."

"It was a worth a shot."

"Yes, good news, folks. A couple adopted Orville's mother a few months before you guys took him."

"Well, this might sound a little odd, but would you be allowed to divulge that information to us—you know, about who took Orville's mom?" asked Vic. "Maybe if Orville and his mom could have a reunion, it would cheer him up."

"Hmm," said the volunteer. "How about I pass your names and phone number on to them, and they can reach out to you?"

"That would be awesome. Thank you so much," said Claudia.

"Sure thing. Since you're here, any chance you want to take a new friend with you?"

"Eh, I think we're good with the ones we have, but thanks," said Vic.

"I understand. Glad I could help, and have a great day."

Vic and Claudia tried one more time to trip up a cat into revealing his or her secrets, this time talking up a cranky-looking orange tabby, but to no avail. Nonetheless, they were successful in their mission, and they were a big step closer to putting a huge smile on Red's heart.

"Hello?"

"Hi. Is this Victor Gioppolo?"

"Yes."

"Hi. My name is Lisa Robinson. I just received a call from someone at the cat shelter who said you were trying to reach me."

"Well, this might sound a little odd, but our cat—his name is Red—is the son of your cat."

"Okay. And . . . ?"

"Well, Red gets a little down sometimes, and"—Vic chuckled nervously—"well, my wife and I were wondering if we could bring Red over to your house for a visit sometime."

There was a pause in the conversation.

"You mean like a cat playdate?" asked Lisa.

"Yes, exactly! And yes, that sounds weird, doesn't it?"

"It does, but I'll allow it." Lisa laughed.

"Oh, thank you so much. That sounds wonderful. We'll bring cat snacks."

"Believe me. That won't be necessary. Aurora has an arsenal of snacks, most of which she ignores. How about next Thursday evening, around 7:00?"

"Perfect. And thank you so much."

"Yes!" said Claudia.

Fatty poked her head around the corner.

"Red's sleeping. What's going on? Is it what I think?"

"Yep, Fatty girl. Red is going to have a reunion with his mom on Thursday. Her name's Aurora."

"Aw, what a nice name. He'll be excited. I'm so happy for him."

"What about you? Do you know of any siblings or parents?"

"I don't remember, Mom. I mean, I kind of have a vague recollection of being alone and suddenly very scared. I must have separated from my family somehow at a young age."

"My gosh. How did you survive out there so young?"

"I don't know. But it's easier now. I'm glad I found you."

"Not half as glad as we are, sweetheart," said Claudia.

"But remember—mum's the word about, well, Red's mom," said Vic.

"What are you looking at?" asked Red, still half asleep, surprised to see Fatty sitting so close to him and staring.

Fatty was so happy for Red's impending good news, she found her eyes locked on her sleepy friend. She quickly recovered.

"The world's most debonair cat, obviously."

"Are you being sincere or mocking me?" asked Red.

"Would it matter?"

"It would not, friend. You know me too well. So, what's on the afternoon agenda?"

"Mom got a package, and not only is there the outside box, but there's an inside product box, too."

"Sweet. Well, what are we waiting for? It's time to sit in new boxes."

VIC COULDN'T KEEP HIS eyes off Red and Fatty as they jumped between the boxes, even sitting together in the larger box, content as cats could be. He had an idea. He grabbed his cellphone and started recording.

"Hey, you two," he said, after recording their antics for several minutes, "come here a second."

They hopped out of the boxes and did as they were asked.

"So, what is the deal with cats and boxes, anyway?" he asked, still recording.

Red: Are you kidding me, Papa? Boxes are the best.

Fatty: It's true. Back when I lived outside, finding an empty box always made me happy. I felt safer and invisible.

Vic: Okay, Fatty girl, that makes sense, but who are you hiding from now?

Fatty: No one. It's just fun. We can pretend.

Red: Yep. When we were both in the big box? We were astronauts.

Vic: Oh, really? Where'd you go?

Red: Mars, of course, Papa. It's the red planet!

Vic: And what did you guys do on Mars?

Fatty: Not much, to be honest. It's kinda boring there. And cold. We aren't fans of the cold.

Red: But we looked cool in our astronaut outfits, no doubt.

Fatty: Cat-ronaut outfits, Red. Don't forget.

Red: Oh, of course, friend. And when we were in separate boxes, it was a train.

Vic: Ah, I see. Go anywhere special?

Red: Nowhere special, Papa. I just—well, I just pretended I took a trip to see my mom. It was nice to think about.

Fatty: And we also took a train trip to the famous and imaginary Catnip Forest.

Vic: Oh, I bet that was fun.

Red: It was. We pretended we filled our suitcases with fresh catnip.

Vic: Do you guys know you have a kindred cardboard spirit in Luca? He made a T. Rex out of cardboard that was on the wall of our stairs for the longest time. And he even made a King Tut sarcophagus when school was canceled for a few days in the winter.

Fatty: We may need to include him in our next adventure.

Red: You know, if you stack the boxes, it could be a double-decker bus. Does Luca have any interest in seeing England?

Vic: He might. You'll have to ask him. Any more words about boxes?

Red: They're all good.

Fatty: Yep, the small ones are good for snuggling. The big ones are good for travel. We can hide in them. We can nap in them.

Red: Whatever humans buy for us, the box the product came in is almost always better.

Fatty: So, just buy us empty boxes. It'll save you money.

Vic: Thanks for the tip.

It was early Thursday evening. Claudia had just gotten home from work. She and Vic knew they were about to make Red the happiest cat on Earth, but they were still trying to figure out how they could transport him to Lisa and Keith's without arousing suspicion. They couldn't think of a good story, so they settled on the direct approach.

"Hey, Reddy, how about you, Claudia, and me take a little trip?"

Red was instantly suspicious.

"Why? Where? Are you taking me back to the shelter? Is this about the clock on the bookshelf? It's nothing a little glue can't fix."

"No, I promise you you're not going back to the—What about the clock on the bookshelf?"

"Uh, nothing, Papa. It might have been Fatty."

"She's kind of earthbound, Red. I doubt she had anything to do with whatever you're talking about."

"Okay, what about Luca, then?" asked Red.

Claudia snuck into the living room to see what happened to the small, delicate clock that sat harmlessly on the bookshelf. Somehow, it now lay in several pieces on the floor.

"Dang it, Red. No, I doubt it was Luca. Why would he do such a thing?" asked Claudia.

"Maybe Papa? He gets mad at work sometimes. I hear him grumbling. Maybe he went Godzilla on the bookshelf."

"Red, buddy, I can assure you it wasn't me."

"Why do you do these things, Red?" asked Claudia.

"It was an accident, honest. I hopped up on the shelf, and the second hand intrigued me. I just wanted to touch it, and, then, before you knew it, boom, crash time."

Claudia sighed. "Be more careful. You know, before we knew your secret, there was really no way to reprimand you. But now?"

"I'm sorry, Mama. Maybe you should punish me by not taking me wherever you and Papa are taking me."

Vic and Claudia exchanged a quick glance and tried not to laugh.

"Reddy boy, just trust us, okay? We're going to take a little trip to a house about five minutes from here. You will like where we're going."

Red agreed and hopped in the carrier for the short car ride to Lisa and Keith's. He sought out assurance from Fatty that nothing funny was going on, and Fatty reminded him how he had steered her right when she was hesitant to come inside the house.

The Gioppolos were greeted by a young couple who welcomed them in. They let Red out of the carrier, and, in the most happily shocking moment of his life, there stood his mom. He knew it was her the second she walked into the room. Vic and Claudia told him that it was very important for him to behave as a normal cat, so he knew that what he wanted to do more than anything—yell "Mom!"—was out of the question.

So, he did the next-best thing. He jumped into her arms, and their momentum carried them away from the humans.

"Gosh, I think you were right about Red," said Lisa.

As the humans made small talk, the cats got reacquainted.

"Mom," said Red in a whisper, "I can't believe it's you. I think about you all the time."

"Orville, my little boy, you have no idea how I wished for this day. Lisa and Keith—that's my humans—were talking about this call they got about some cat named Red, and I put the pieces together and figured it was you. I could hardly sleep or eat for the past few days."

"Yes, Red is my name now. And it's a long story, but my humans know our secret."

Aurora gasped. "You're kidding. How did they react?"

"Well, there was almost a car wreck because Fatty"—

"Fatty? Who's Fatty?"

"Oh, the other cat in the house. She's awesome."

"Wait. She has the gift, too?"

"Yes. It's weird, right? She wandered into the backyard one day, and I gently persuaded her to join the family. What's your name now?"

"Aurora."

"Oh, that's nice, Mom."

They both stopped and stared at each other, still amazed they were sharing the same room again. They both were thinking about that sad day at the shelter, when they were separated and whispering what they assumed would be their last goodbyes.

The humans were continuing their pleasant chit-chat, with Lisa and Keith feeling assured that Vic's story was legit, seeing how the cats were getting along so well.

"Are your humans nice, honey?"

"Are you kidding? Mama and Papa and the boy—that's their son, Luca—are the best. How about yours?"

"They're terrific. They both work during the day, so the weekdays can be pretty lonely, but they shower me with attention in the evenings and weekends. I'm very lucky."

"We have to do this all the time, Mom. You need to meet the boy. And Fatty! You'll love Fatty."

Mother and son both realized it would help them get repeat play-dates if they sauntered over to the humans and showed how well-behaved they were.

"Honey, look at Aurora," said Lisa. "I swear she's beaming. I have to admit, Vic. I thought your request was a little, well, odd."

"Yeah, I don't blame you. But we haven't seen Red this happy in a while. We can't thank you enough for letting us visit with him."

"Oh, anytime," said Keith. "They seem to be getting along with no problems."

"Next time, maybe Aurora would like to visit us?" said Claudia.

"I don't think she'd mind at all," said Lisa.

And the two then scampered off out of earshot to continue their conversation.

"Did you hear that? You're invited to my house. It's gonna be awesome."

"I can't wait, Orville. Or should I say Red?"

"You can call me anything you like, Mom. This is the happiest day of my life."

They butted heads one final time, as Vic called for Red to hop back in his carrier.

"Again, I can't thank you enough. Just call us soon so that we can return the favor and host lovely Aurora," said Vic.

"We will. This was so nice for them, and it was great meeting you."

They were safely in the car and out of view of the Robinsons when Red let loose with a torrent of words.

"Mama, Papa, you're the best! How did you locate my mother? She's awesome! I never thought I'd see her again. Can she come over tomorrow? Maybe we can have sleepovers? I can't wait for Fatty to meet my mom!"

"Are you happy, Red? Well, you've mentioned missing your mom a few times, to us and Fatty, so we decided to pay a visit to the shelter to see if we could track your mother down," said Vic. "We were happy to find out that she was adopted by a family close by. Lisa contacted me, and well, here we are."

"Now I have two moms, Mama. I'm a lucky boy."

"You are, Reddy. And, yes, we will set up a home playdate for Aurora. She's welcome anytime."

"When you were at the shelter, you didn't happen to see an angry-looking orange dude, did you?"

"Well, yeah, actually," said Claudia. "We were trying to see if any of the other cats shared your and Fatty's gift, and we did notice an orange cat who seemed none too pleased to be engaged with."

"Ah, Sunset. I wonder how many times he's been returned to the shelter since I left."

"So, Red, we're kind of assuming that Aurora talks, too?" asked Claudia.

"Yes. That's why we scurried away. But her humans don't know."

"Don't worry. We won't say anything," said Vic. "And she can let her guard down when she visits."

"This is the best day ever, Mama and Papa. Thank you so much for finding my mom."

"We're happy for you, Reddy," said Vic.

"But we didn't forget about the clock, pal," said Claudia.

"Are—are you going to tell my mom?"

"No, Red. She can't punish you. But we can," said Claudia. "No snacks for two days. And behave!"

Red sighed. "I'm sorry about the clock. But this is still the best day ever."

Fatty was resting on the dining-room rug, listening to Luca practice his guitar. He was playing the same song repeatedly, trying to perfect it for his upcoming recital. Fatty found herself humming along and picking up the beat as the song sounded better with each pass.

"What's the name of the song, Luca?" she asked.

"It's called 'Blue Skies.'"

"Does it have words?"

"It does, Fatty."

"Mind if I sing along with some made-up words?"

"Sure. I didn't know you sang."

"I didn't, either, Luca, but here goes."

Luca picked it up from the beginning, this time accompanied by a singing Fatty.

> Blue skies up in the sky
> Where else would they be?
> My, oh, my
>
> Blue skies, here comes a bird
> Better watch out
> 'Cause now I've stirred
>
> Luca plays guitar
> Red's in the car
> Meeting his mom
> Having some fun
>
> Blue car on the road
> Mom and Kind Sir
> and the one with fur

Luca's nailed this song
I'm singing along
I made up the words
I won't be deterred

Blue bowl filled with food
Now I gotta run
My job here's done

They both had a good laugh over Fatty's made-up words.

"You're funny, Fatty."

"Thanks, Luca. And you're nice."

"Why wouldn't I be?"

"I don't know. I guess I'm still amazed that humans can be nice. Anyway, I can't wait to hear Red's stories when he comes home. Did you hear his mom's name is Aurora?"

"I did, Fatty."

"That's such a nice name."

Fatty stopped talking, and Luca was confused before realizing what she was getting at.

"You know, buddy, when I gave you your name, we had no idea you talked or understood what we were saying. I wouldn't have done that to you had I known."

"I know, Luca. It wasn't done with mean intent. It's just . . ."

"I can talk to Mom and Dad if you'd like. Maybe you can be—what's that word Dad likes to use?—rebranded."

"I'd like that, Luca. Thank you. So, what kind of guitar is that, anyway?"

"It's called an acoustic guitar. But what I really want is an electric one."

"Ah, so you can be a rock star, right? What's it called?"

"A Fender Stratocaster. The one I want is red and white. It's sweet."

"Well, maybe I'll drop a word to Santa Cat."

Luca wasn't sure if Fatty was kidding.

"Wait. That's not a thing, is it, Fatty?"

"What? You never heard of Santa Cat? Every Catmas Eve, he loads a giant cardboard sleigh with cardboard boxes of various sizes for all the good cat boys and cat girls around the world."

Seeing how he was having a conversation with a talking cat, who just accompanied him on vocals while he played his guitar, Luca truly didn't know what to believe anymore when it came to felines. He gave Fatty an expressionless stare.

"Yes, Luca, I'm kidding."

And they were both giggling again as the rest of their family returned home, with Red all but bursting out of his carrier and the words spilling from his tongue as fast he could form them.

"Fatty, bro, I met my mom again. It was awesome! Her name's Aurora. She has nice humans, too! Their names are Lisa and Keith. She's coming over for a playdate because she lives pretty close by. I can't wait for you to meet her."

"I'm happy for you, Red," said Fatty.

"Oh, and she talks, too, but her humans don't know. So be a normal cat when they're around. We know what almost happened last time you blurted out the truth, Fatty."

"Red, one of you would have slipped up eventually," Vic said.

"Yeah, you're probably right. But don't forget that Fatty darn near caused a 27-car pileup that would have certainly made national news, with you being carted off to prison muttering, 'But—but the cats talk. You have to believe me.' The whole country would have thought you were a lunatic. Lunatic Vic. Think about it, Papa. Rhyming nicknames stick."

"Red, that might be a wee bit of an embellishment, don't you think?" said Vic.

"Don't sweat it, Fatty," said Claudia. "Red's just cranky because we've given him a two-day snack reprieve for the clock incident. Oh, by the way, Fatty, would you like some snacks?"

"You're cold-hearted, Mama," said Red.

"Yeah, Reddy, I'm a monster."

"Anything new here, sport?" asked Vic.

"No, I was just practicing for the recital. And Fatty was my vocalist."

"She was? Well, you'll have to sing for all of us sometime, Fatty."

"Maybe. I don't know if I could sing in front of a crowd."

"I love a crowd, bro. Maybe I could learn the drums?"

"Yeah, that probably isn't the best idea, Red," said Vic.

"Man, no snacks, no drum. You guys are the worst. You're also the best for finding my mom."

"You sound a little confused, Red," said Fatty.

"I am, friend. I'm also tired. It's been an eventful day. Well, I'm off to bed—without snacks, of course."

"Good night, Reddy," said Claudia as he scampered off to bed. "I'm glad you got to see your mom again."

"Fatty girl, you should have seen Red and his mom. I don't know how they kept their talking so low," said Vic. "They were so excited."

"Well, we do have excellent hearing, so a whisper would do the trick. I'm happy for him, and I can't wait to meet Aurora."

"Yeah, we'll have to set up the date soon for her to visit because you know Red will be asking us every ten minutes," said Claudia.

"Well, my singing debut has made me pretty tired, too. I'm off to bed."

"Good night, sweetheart," said Claudia. "And thanks for telling us about Red's desire to see his mom."

Fatty was ready to jump into her cat bed, but before she did, she got up close to Red's left ear and whispered, "I'm happy for you, buddy. And I might have a left a snack or two for you in the kitchen."

"You're the best, pal. We cats have to stick together."

A FEW DAYS BEFORE the Fourth of July, Franklin received the call he'd been expecting.

"Hey, Dad. It's Martin. You want to come over for a cookout?"

Franklin knew Martin was expecting a terse "No," followed by a few perfunctory exchanges, and then his son could return to his life and explain to his wife and sisters that he offered Dad an invitation, but he said no. They'd all feign sadness and simultaneously breathe a sigh of relief, knowing they'd have one fewer headache to be concerned about.

"You know what, Martin? Sure. I'd like to see you and the grandkids."

"That's great, Dad. Just, uh, promise us you won't start partying too early."

There was silence.

"Did you forget I was a full-grown adult, son? Remember when I taught you how to throw a curveball or drive a car? When I need your advice, I'll ask for it."

Click.

There was regret on both ends.

"Why do we even bother inviting the old fool?" Martin yelled to his wife.

"He said no?" asked Beth.

Martin sighed. "No, he said yes, but when I ever so gently asked him not to start drinking before he got here, he reminded me that he was an adult and that he taught me how to throw a baseball."

Beth embraced her husband. "I remember a different Franklin. And I know you and your sisters do, too. That man is still there. We just have to find him."

Franklin added his response to Martin to his ever-growing pile of regrets. He knew teaching his son how to drive or the fundamentals of baseball had nothing to do with his current predicament. Yet confronting the truth was too painful. He couldn't do it. If the truth hurts, the pain must be numbed. Franklin had the perfect prescription.

As he sat in his favorite chair, drinking the night away while staring blankly at whatever the TV offered, he promised himself that he would behave on the Fourth. He fell asleep cocooned in the pleasant thought of impressing his children and grandchildren with the new-and-improved Franklin as his empty tumbler slipped slowly from his hand and landed gently on the carpet.

He awoke several hours later to the sounds of some fading actor promoting reverse mortgages, picked up his glass, and stumbled off to bed, much less sure of the promise he made to himself only hours earlier.

INDEPENDENCE DAY. FRANKLIN AWOKE slightly buzzed from the night before. In fact, he wasn't sure he had spent any moment of the past few days sober. After he vowed to behave for his son's cookout, he doubled down on his disease, fully indulging it, ignoring all the guardrails. And since it was Independence Day, he was declaring independence from common sense.

He showered, brushed his teeth, and doused his breath with an ungodly amount of mouthwash to kill off any scent of whiskey. He was a veteran of the drinking game. He could pass as sober when Martin or Beth swung by to pick him up. But he knew what he had in store for his family. After all, what's the Fourth without fireworks?

It was Beth who picked him up. Franklin had known her since she was a young adult. She was a good wife, a good mother, a good person. Franklin always liked her. But the state of mind he was in didn't allow for anything positive to find daylight.

"Franklin, I'm so glad you could join us today," Beth said as he entered the car.

"Uh-huh," said Franklin.

"Martin hates the thought of you being alone on holidays. And the kids can't wait to see you."

"Is that so?"

"It's great weather for a cookout. Hope you brought your appetite."

"Sure."

The conversation continued like this for several minutes, with Beth asking questions and Franklin replying as curtly as possible. If this were a job interview, Beth thought, Franklin most definitely would not be getting a callback.

Eventually, Beth gave up trying to initiate conversation, and they drove in silence the rest of the way until they reached the driveway.

Beth shut off the ignition and said, "Franklin, let your grandchildren see the real you, the version of you I remember when I first started dating your son. We deserve better. More importantly, you deserve better. We love you, Franklin."

Beth's words were perfect. Part of Franklin knew it. But what Beth didn't know was that Franklin was already two-thirds of the way into becoming the angry drunk. He faced a choice. Eat something, sober up, and live up to Beth's noble words. Or have a few more drinks and put on a show for the family. He remained in the car, weighing his options.

"Don't be afraid, Franklin. This can be the first day of the rest of your life. And we're all here for you—even Ruth. She's never left your side."

The mention of his late wife's name was Beth's final touch, and Franklin exited the car feeling better than he had in years. He would do it. Starting right now.

He entered the kitchen and felt a series of tentatively spoken "Hellos" wash over him. He knew what his reputation was. But today would be different. Nobody would have to walk on eggshells in his presence ever again.

And then Martin handed him a can of pop and whispered, "Behave."

And that was it. While Beth's words struck the right note, Martin's admonition returned Franklin to Plan "A." He would not tolerate such insolence from a child of his. The show would proceed as originally planned.

He took the pop and said nothing, but when Martin left the room, Franklin spiked the cola with the first bottle of booze he could reach. Cola and gin may not have been a conventional drink, but it did the job, and Franklin's thirst for independence was sated temporarily.

There was a good crowd at the house, and with everyone being occupied by conversation or volleyball or kids running around, it was easy for Franklin to casually slip in a second, third, and fourth drink.

Even Martin, who knew his warning would likely be unheeded, was concentrating on the grill and enduring well-meaning advice from numerous friends and neighbors about the proper way to barbecue burgers.

So, no one noticed Franklin's increasing state of inebriation. And while Beth and Martin had the sense to keep the holiday sparklers and lighter out of the reach of the children, Franklin had no trouble grabbing both off the fireplace mantel.

So, as the games and the grilling and the jovial talking continued, no one noticed a drunk, old man brandishing sparklers as he entered the backyard. And no one noticed when he tripped over a badminton racket and began falling to the ground.

But everyone noticed when the paper tablecloth covering the picnic table ignited and quickly engulfed everything within reach. And everyone heard Michaela's screams as the sleeve of her blouse caught fire.

Beth flew through the air like a linebacker and tackled her daughter, dousing the blouse's flames. A quick-thinking neighbor grabbed a nearby garden hose and showered the table, reinforced by Martin, who was brandishing a kitchen fire extinguisher.

The young ones were yelling and crying. The adults were shaken but putting on brave faces for their kids. Half the crowd had called 911, so the fire company was there, with their trucks' deafening sirens bringing out the entire neighborhood.

And at the center of it all sat Franklin, quietly weeping and clutching a box of sparklers.

Beth and Martin hopped in the ambulance with their daughter. "Get him out of here!" was all Martin could say to his sister Jane before departing.

"Let's get you home, Dad," said Jane.

Franklin assented to his daughter's words, but he could feel everyone's eyes boring holes into him.

The car ride was quiet until Jane could no longer hold her tongue.

"What on Earth were you thinking, Dad?"

"It was an accident. I didn't mean to—"

"But you're drunk. Again. And you thought parading outside with lit sparklers was a good idea?"

"You know, on the way here, your sister-in-law spoke such beautiful words. Today was going to be different. And then your brother just had to open his mouth."

"He loves you, Dad. We all do."

"Yeah, I don't know about that. You want to know what he said to me?"

"Sure, Dad. What did he say?"

"He told me to behave. Like I'm a child. How dare he. How dare any of you."

"So, you were so incensed at Martin for talking to you like a child that you decided to behave like a child who suddenly found a lighter?"

"Oh, so, you, too, huh? I'm your father!"

"And your granddaughter is in the emergency room. And you could have killed people. Accidents happen to all of us. But not all of us are drunks. You are, Dad."

The rest of the trip was silent. Jane helped her father get inside his house, encouraged him to go directly to bed, and left.

Beth's quick thinking saved her daughter from serious injury or worse. It took an emergency-room doctor little time to clean and bandage Michaela's burn, but she would have a souvenir scar on her upper right arm for the rest of her life and a story for anyone willing to listen of how not to conduct yourself.

"Why can't you guys force Grandpa to get help?" said Michaela on the way home.

"He's an adult, honey. There's no way we can force him to do anything," said Martin.

"I really thought I convinced him, Martin," said Beth. "He didn't say anything, but I could tell my words had an impact, especially when I mentioned your mother."

"I screwed up, Beth. You told me what you told him. Your words were perfect. I shouldn't have said anything when I saw him."

"What did you say to him, Martin?"

"I handed him a pop and told him to behave. What was I thinking?"

"Honey, you're not responsible for what your father did. He could have killed our daughter or heaven knows how many people. His stupidity could have unleashed a catastrophe. Do not blame yourself."

"He's my father, Beth. Someday Michaela might find herself in a similar situation with us. How would you like taking orders from her?"

"I eagerly await the day," said Michaela.

Martin and Beth chuckled. They needed a laugh after witnessing hurricane-force idiocy unleashed in their backyard.

"What do we do now, Beth? I want to drive over there this instant and yell till my voice grows hoarse. I also want to hug him and beg him to seek help."

Martin punched the steering wheel in exasperation.

"I wish you could have known my real father, Michaela. He was my role model. There was no one I admired more."

It was true. Franklin Betters grew up poor but excelled academically. As a 19-year-old, he found himself in a faraway land, serving his country. He rose to the rank of captain, and after the conflict ended in

Korea, he took advantage of a government-instituted program offering a college education for returning soldiers.

He studied business at a local university, graduated with honors, fell in love, got married, and opened a one-man insurance company, which over time would grow and prosper, enabling Franklin to give his wife and children the kind of life he could only dream about as a child.

At 30, he and Ruth welcomed their first child, a healthy baby boy, into the world. They named him Martin, after Martin Luther King, who at the time was opening the nation's eyes to centuries of racial injustice. They admired the reverend deeply and hoped their son would always follow a righteous path and be a force of good in the world.

Two more children, both daughters, quickly followed, and the Betters family lived a picture-perfect life. Though often busy working, Franklin always found time for his children, whether it was coaching baseball or softball or attending violin recitals or gymnastics meets.

None of Franklin and Ruth's children remember their parents arguing, because when any conflict arose—as they inevitably do—the parents took matters behind closed doors and found resolution to the problem without raising their voices.

And none of Franklin and Ruth's children remember their parents being drunk, either. Sure, there would occasionally be an after-work drink or wine with dinner, but the only time any of the children saw their father even tipsy was after the Steelers won their first Super Bowl. But the only result of that was some happy yelling and driveway horn honking, which the three kids and everyone else in the neighborhood accompanied with pot-banging and harmless mayhem.

Franklin wasn't the type of father to sit his children down and lecture them. Rather, he led by example, planting seeds in their heads every day about how one should conduct his life. The three children all paid attention, excelling through their teens and into early adulthood. And when Jane, their youngest, was set to embark on her post-collegiate life, Franklin and Ruth were ready to set forth on their long-awaited European adventure, which they had been meticulously planning for months.

And then, of course, the tragedy of Franklin's life occurred, and for the past two decades he's been a different man.

His problem started out innocently enough—a drink here and there, maybe one before bed to help him sleep and ease the pain. At first, the kids didn't say anything, because they were processing their own grief at the sudden loss of their mother and because they couldn't imagine how their father could cope with such tragedy. Their parents loved each other, of course. But they never fell out of love, either, forever holding hands or dropping romantic notes around the house for one another.

But the problem escalated, slowly and steadily, and whenever one of the kids would try, tentatively, to broach the subject with their father, they would be quickly shut down and told the problem was under control.

They knew the man of character their father was. They wanted to give him wide berth on the matter, considering his well-earned reputation. They wanted to believe he would solve the situation himself and on his own terms. They were waiting for a day when he would admit he had a problem, get help, if necessary, and return to the man he had been—a sadder version, certainly, but the man they used to know.

He didn't. He couldn't. The disease was winning and kept making advances, diminishing the good man for all to witness. At some point, he became Old Man Bitters, the neighborhood cur. If the Ghost of Franklin's Future could have shown him in, say, 1987, what would become of him, he surely would have been as dismissive as old Ebenezer Scrooge had been. "An undigested bit of beef," indeed.

As the disease progressed, the visits and calls from his children grew more infrequent. The man they constantly went to for advice became the unreliable cannon in each of their lives. Their own children dreaded Grandpa's visits, knowing they would usually result in a scene of some sort, particularly the holidays. Without warning, it would suddenly be time for Grandpa to go home, before he did something worse than falling asleep during dinner or slurring unintelligibly.

Martin and his sisters did their best to shield the children from Franklin's drunken antics and were largely successful until Independence Day, which was bad enough but could have been so much worse. Sure, their daughter's injury would take some time to heal, and no doubt the flashbacks of her peril would last even longer, and sure, they'd have to apologize to their neighbors for the chaos that descended upon their usually quiet neighborhood. But the damage to their yard was minimal, no one else was injured, and the neighbors would forgive them and dismiss it as a one-time occurrence.

And perhaps, they thought, something good would emerge from the event. Perhaps Franklin had finally learned his lesson. Maybe this was finally rock bottom, and he would pick himself up off the mat and be the Franklin Betters his kids remembered and his grandkids never met.

AND FOR A FEW days, that's what began to happen. A half-dozen times, Franklin picked up the phone to apologize to Martin and to see how his granddaughter was doing. But he just couldn't do it. He was ashamed of the mayhem he was entirely responsible for. He couldn't bear to even hear his son's voice. But he had been sober, at least.

The third day after the incident, however, he convinced himself that just one little drink would take the edge off and help him make the phone call he knew he had to make. So, he poured a shot of whiskey into a glass and tossed in an ice cube or two. Just one little drink. Just to steady himself. Apologizing is never easy, especially when it's accompanied by deep remorse. My goodness, what would Ruth think of what he had become? This wasn't the man she married and had loved every day of their lives together.

Ahh. It felt good, and it did steady him. But instead of picking up the phone and doing what needed to be done, he figured another one would make his task even easier.

And before he knew it, he was on the floor and sobbing, with half a bottle of whiskey sloshing around his gullet. Tomorrow. He would call tomorrow, he promised himself.

But tomorrow came and played out largely the same as today had. All the days had a numbing repetition to them. And now, further compounding his malaise was the fact that not only was he a drunk, but he had yet to call to see how his granddaughter was feeling—the granddaughter he almost killed because of his senselessness.

This was not lost on Martin, who was not only angry at his father but also hurt by the lack of communication.

"He's embarrassed, Martin. Maybe you should call him?"

"He should be embarrassed, Beth. And no, I'm not going to call him. It's on him to reach out to us. Remember that time he almost killed our daughter and could have killed or injured who knows how many of our guests? Do you want me to point out the scorch marks in our yard, in case you've forgotten?"

Martin exhaled.

"I'm sorry, Beth. I'm beyond frustrated."

"I know. I'm as frustrated as you are. But should we be concerned?"

So, weeks passed. Neither side would budge. The phone sat silent. Franklin had now grown indignant that none of his children had called him. The Fourth of July incident apparently was not rock bottom.

Franklin still had some digging to do.

RED AWOKE EARLIER THAN normal. He was excited because Aurora was coming over for a playdate, and he wanted everything to be perfect.

Claudia and Vic awoke earlier than they wanted to, seeing how it was Saturday. Yet there was their 11-pound orange-and-white cat, staring them into wakefulness at the foot of their bed.

"Something wrong, Reddy?" asked Claudia.

"Nope. Everything's great. I'm just excited about Mom coming over, and I want everything to be just right."

"Would you like us to vacuum and dust and bring out the good china?" asked Vic.

"Well, if it wouldn't be a bother."

"Red, your mom will be very happy to see you and to meet Fatty. I doubt she'll care if there's some dust on the bookshelf. Go back to sleep," said Claudia.

"If you'd like, I could jump all over the bookshelf and give it a thorough dusting—no charge."

"And you could end up knocking over heaven knows what in the process. Would you like to go snackless for the rest of your life?" asked Claudia.

"Point made, Mama. I just want Mom to get the best impression. Can Fatty and I have a brushing before she gets here?"

"Sure, as long as you let us go back to sleep."

"Would you like to wear a little cat suit and tie, too, Red?" asked Vic.

"Well, if you think it'd be best, then—"

"Goodbye, Reddy."

"Got it, Papa."

Red scampered off. It wasn't quite 7:30, Aurora wasn't arriving until 2:00, and Vic and Claudia were now wide awake.

"Well, we're not going back to sleep, are we? Maybe I'll go for a jog, Claud."

"When's the last time you went jogging, honey?"

"Uh, let's see. I was 19, maybe 20."

"You think it's a good idea to just plunge back into jogging after a few decades' absence?"

"Well, you know what they say. There's no time like the present."

But before Vic could get on his sneakers, in came Luca.

"Red just woke me up. He told me I should be at my most polite today when his mom visits."

Vic chuckled.

"Yeah, buddy, he wants his mom to have a nice visit. It's cute that he's nervous, but he doesn't need to be. We'll all just be ourselves. I'm sure Aurora will be fine with it."

"Remember the other day when Fatty was singing for me?" asked Luca.

His parents nodded.

"Well, she told me something that I promised her I'd pass on to you. She doesn't like her name, and I explained that I never would have called her that if I knew she understood what we were saying."

"That's sweet of you to tell her that, Luca. And thank you for letting us know," said Claudia.

"So, Fatty girl wants a rebranding, eh? I think we could probably work something out," said Vic.

Luca laughed.

"I told her you'd say something like that. Thanks, Mom and Dad."

"Hey, buddy, let's say you and I take a little trip to the home store while Red visits with his mom."

"Okay, Dad. Sounds good."

"Still going for that jog?"

"No, Claud. I have an even better idea. You'll see."

As 2:00 approached, Red went from room to room, making sure nothing was out of place. The rest of the family enjoyed the spectacle. Red finally sensed four sets of eyes staring through him.

"What? She's my mom. I want her to feel comfortable here."

Finally, before Red morphed into a drill sergeant, the doorbell rang.

"Lisa, please come in. It's nice to see you again."

"Likewise, Claudia."

"And hello, again, Aurora."

Lisa chuckled.

"It's funny. We usually have a bear of a time getting her into this thing. But today? She all but jumped in. It's as if she knew where she was going."

Vic and Claudia joined Lisa in her amusement, before Vic recovered and said, "Excuse me, Lisa, but Luca and I have an errand to run. It was nice seeing you again."

"Same, Vic."

"Hi, Mrs. Robinson. I'm Luca. It's nice to meet you."

"Oh, hello, young man. It's nice meeting you, too."

"Okay, you two, off to your mystery chore," said Claudia. "Lisa, I just made coffee if you'd like. We can catch up while the cats do whatever it is cats do on a playdate."

"Sounds wonderful, Claudia."

While Claudia and Lisa immersed themselves in conversation, the cats snuck off to the living room, out of earshot.

"Mom, this is my pal Fatty. Fatty, this is my mom."

"Aurora, it's such a pleasure to meet you. And that's such a pretty name," said Fatty.

"Thank you. It's nice meeting you, too. Red told me so much about you when we met."

"So, this is the living room, Mom. These are our beds, which we sleep in occasionally. Come on. Let us show you around."

And off they went, touring each room. When they walked through the kitchen, Lisa couldn't help but laugh.

"Is Red a real estate agent, Claudia? Don't forget to mention the granite countertops, Red."

"Once you get to know him, you'll notice that he has quite the personality," said Claudia, hoping that Red wouldn't slip up and reveal his true self.

As they departed the kitchen and were in the safe zone again, Fatty gave Red a warning.

"Red, don't forget that Aurora's human doesn't know our secret. Tone it down."

"Fatty, I can't just turn off my personality. But don't worry. I won't blow it. Which reminds me—Mom, did I ever tell you the story of how Fatty almost caused a 50-car pileup when she started talking to Papa in a moving car?"

"Red, does this story get a little more outlandish with each telling, or is it just me?" asked Fatty.

"Yes, son, you told me when we met at my house. But I don't remember it involving 50 cars."

Aurora patted Red on the head and laughed.

"Son, you've always had such a charming way about you. I'm glad you found nice humans and a wonderful friend in Fatty."

"And watch this, Mom."

And like a shot, Red darted into the kitchen, built up speed in the hallway and leapt through the air, landing atop the living-room bookshelf.

Lisa and Claudia put down their coffee and followed Red into the living room.

"Oh, he must be a handful, Claudia," said Lisa.

"You have no idea. Okay, Reddy, you can come down now. There are no zebras on the savannah. I'm sure your mother is impressed."

Red did as he was told, and the two humans returned to their coffee.

"What did you think, Mom?"

"Well, that's impressive, but you need to listen to your humans. They've given you a loving home."

"Aw, don't worry. They're cool with my antics."

"Really, Red? I'm pretty sure I remember someone being on a snack time-out just the other—"

"Eh, stop, Fatty. Mom doesn't want to hear about that. Let's race into Luca's room."

And so the three of them went flying up the stairs to see who was fastest. And then they tore back downstairs because they realized how fun it was. And then they returned to Luca's room and decided it was a good time for a nap.

Before it was time to go, Lisa and Claudia made arrangements for future get-togethers.

"They get along so well. It's nice to see. Honestly, bring Aurora over anytime. It's not like they need supervision. We could even go to lunch together and leave our furry friends alone."

"I like the sound of that, Claudia. Okay, Aurora, in you go."

Red furtively waved bye to his mom, but unlike their parting at the shelter, he knew he'd see her again.

"What are you two up to?" said Claudia to her husband and son.

"Well, we went to the home store and bought wood. And with that wood, we're going to make a sign."

"Ah, I get it. You're going to put a giant sign in the front yard that says, 'Home of the Famous Talking Cats. $10 adults, $5 kids and senior citizens.'"

"No," said Vic, "but that is an appealing thought."

"It's for Fatty, Mom."

Claudia gave them a quizzical look.

"She hates her name. Remember?" said Luca.

"So," continued Vic, "we're going to figure out what her new name is, and we're going to make a sign to put above her bed so that everyone knows it."

"That's sweet, you two."

"Where are the two little furballs, anyway?"

"Last I saw they were in the spare bedroom. They were running around with Aurora, so I'm guessing that wore them out."

And at that moment, Claudia was proved wrong, as the cats came tearing into the room, in the middle of a spirited discussion.

"Stop calling me Fatty. That can't be my real name."

"So, what is your real name, then?"

"I don't know. What's yours?"

"It's Red. Duh."

"No, your real name. That's the name our humans gave you. What's your real name?"

"It's Red."

Fatty sighed. "No, your real—Oh, I bet it's something horrible. Is it . . . Horace?"

"No."

"Cletus?"

"No."

"Burt."

"No!"

"Oh, my gosh, it's Burt, isn't it . . . 'Red'?" She did air quotes as she said "Red."

"Shut up, Fatty!"

"Burt!"

"Fatty!"

"Burt!"

"Fatty!"

"Enough, both of you!" shouted Vic. "What's this all about, anyway?"

"Red's real name is Burt, sir. He just told me."

"It is not!"

"Actually," Vic began to say, "at the shelter, it was—"

"That's not important right now," shouted Red. "This is how rumors start!"

"Well, now you know how I feel! Maybe I have a pretty-girl name, like Jasmine or, I don't know, Rebecca or something."

And then Fatty darted out of the room, embarrassed she was part of such a scene.

All eyes were on Red.

"She keeps talking about what a nice name my mom has. I guess she's not crazy about the name you guys gave her."

"Would you be?" asked Claudia.

Red shook his head.

"Red, Luca explained to her that he never would have given her that name—and we never would have agreed to it—had any of us known you guys were capable of comprehending everything we say," said Vic.

"Yeah, I understand. It's just . . . I'll go talk to her," said Red.

"And, Luca, you and I have some building to do. It looks as though our dear Fatty is about to be rebranded as Jasmine."

Red poked his head around the corner of the spare bedroom.

"Hey, buddy, do you want to talk about it?"

"I wasn't always this shape, you know," said Fatty.

"No, I know. You almost starved out there. And then our humans took you in and fed you, and since you have to do a lot less chasing now, well, you became a little rounder."

Fatty chuckled.

"That's a polite way to put it."

"But here's the thing," said Red. "You're not a Jasmine or a Rebecca or a Marisol or whatever other name you think is a better fit. You're sweet and funny and good-hearted. You're Fatty, and I . . . well, I'm quite fond of you."

"I'm . . . fond of you, too, Red, but it's a ridiculous name."

"No, it isn't. It's you. It's a term of endearment. It's adorable. You're everyone's favorite three-legged, portly cat. When I was at the shelter, I forget how many times I was overlooked. It hurt. I felt rejected. But eventually those good humans in the other room chose me, and then they chose you. They accepted us as we were. Can you accept yourself, friend?"

Fatty was speechless. She never heard Red speak so candidly.

"You're awesome just the way you are, Fatty."

Meanwhile, Claudia was admiring Vic and Luca's handiwork.

"Don't look at me, Claud. My father was a cabinetmaker, you know, but, as they say, talent skips a generation. Most of this was the boy's handiwork. I merely supervised and made sure he didn't lop off a hand."

"Yeah, you don't read about too many one-handed guitar players, do you?" she asked.

The three of them had just about hung up the brightly painted "M" above the newly branded Jasmine's bed when Fatty burst into the room.

"That's very kind of you all, but I'm not a Jasmine or a Rebecca. I'm Fatty, and I embrace who I am."

And she turned with her tail high and scampered off.

The three of them sat there and didn't know what to say.

"Whatever Red said must have been pretty awesome," said Vic.

"He can be full of himself, but he's a kind-hearted bloke, isn't he?" asked Claudia.

"And don't forget fiendishly handsome, Mama."

"Dang it, Red. You weren't supposed to be hearing our discussion," said Vic.

"Yeah, well, I'm a cat. Did you forget we have exceptional hearing, especially when our name is invoked?"

"You're a good friend, Red," said Claudia.

"I am quite a handsome friend, Mama. You're right. So, what are you going to do with the name sign?"

"Oh, I don't know. Maybe the boy will date a girl named Jasmine someday, and he can present her with a clunky wooden necklace bearing her name," said Vic.

"Don't listen to your father, honey. Most ladies prefer shiny necklaces, not wooden ones."

"Ah, your mother's all wrong, Luca. Nothing touches a young lady's heart more than a handmade gift. It exudes love."

"Yeah, and paint fumes, dear. Don't listen to your father."

"I'm not listening to either of you," said Luca. "I'm never getting married."

Vic and Claudia chuckled.

"Yeah, neither am I," said Red. "We young males have to hold on to our independence." He gave Luca a high five.

"I love our crazy family," said Claudia as she draped the Jasmine necklace around her husband's neck. "Let's never change a thing."

MICHAELA TOOK A DEEP breath and knocked on her grandfather's front door. Her parents were unaware of what she was doing, but she figured the best way to ease the tension in her home was to confront the source directly.

There was no response. She knocked again, this time a little louder. His car was in the driveway. She knew he was in there.

Franklin heard the knocking and tried to ignore it, initially assuming it was a kid selling something he didn't need or a neighbor he didn't wish to see. Then he snuck a peek and realized it was his granddaughter, and he froze, not knowing how to proceed.

He wasn't sure if he was actively drunk, hungover, or, improbably, both simultaneously. If he let her in, he wasn't sure how he'd behave, and he didn't want to scare her more than he already had. But if he continued to ignore her knocking, it would further erode the relationship with Martin. He incorrectly assumed she was being sent as an ambassador by her father.

The knocking continued. He admired her pluck. He approached the door. She had a smile on her face. And when she lifted her arm and offered a friendly wave, he saw the sizable bandage on her arm. He wanted to turn back, but it was too late.

"Grandpa, I was on my way home from work, and I thought I'd come see how you were."

He motioned for her to enter but said nothing.

"So . . . how are you?"

"Did your father send you?"

"No. Mom and Dad don't know I'm here. It's just—"

"What? Out with it."

"Well, Grandpa, you've been the topic of many conversations in my home the past few days, and it seems both you and my father are quite capable of being stubborn."

"He can call me just as easily as I can call him."

"Right. But neither of you are picking up the phone. So, here I am."

Michaela noticed he was standing unsteadily. The last thing she wanted was another scene involving her grandfather.

"Are—are you okay, Grandpa? Maybe we should sit down?"

"Why? You think ol' Grandpa is going to fall down again? Then, what? You can run home to St. Martin and tell him how horrible I am?"

"Grandpa, no. I came here because I genuinely—"

"Go. Just go. I didn't ask for this. I don't need this. I don't need any of you. Just leave me alone."

The easy path for Michaela was to listen to her grandfather and leave promptly. But she came here on a mission. So, she took a deep breath and spoke her mind, regardless of the consequences.

"Grandpa, my parents are the best people I know. They are heartsick about you. I've seen those good people in tears every time they talk about you. You can't go on like this. None of us can." There was a crack in her voice, but she delivered the intended message.

Franklin departed for the kitchen and quickly reappeared, brazenly sipping a whiskey.

"As I said to you a moment ago, Michaela, leave me alone. Unless, of course, you care to join me for a drink?" He chuckled at his own ridiculous joke.

She didn't want to give him the satisfaction of seeing her cry, so she quickly departed and saved her tears for the ride home. She felt foolish for thinking she could make a difference. She thought it would be such a good idea. In the fantasy version, they would have a heart-to-heart discussion. He would express genuine remorse for almost killing her. He might even weep. He would tell her he's been sober since the Fourth and that he was just too ashamed to reach out. She would offer nothing but understanding. They would hug. She'd take him home with her. He would embrace Martin and Beth, admit to his mistakes, tell them that he was on a path to sobriety and that he would take it day by day. There would be a group hug and a clean start, and all would be well in their world.

"He didn't even ask how your arm was?" asked Martin.

The second Michaela entered the house, Martin and Beth knew something was amiss. She told them the whole story and apologized for even trying.

"No, honey, you have nothing to apologize for," said Beth. "It was lovely what you did."

"Did he somehow not see the bandage that goes from your shoulder to your elbow?" asked Martin.

"Dad, I'm sure he saw it. I think that's what made him surly. He saw me at the door, and the second I waved, the look on his face changed instantly."

"He feels incredible shame, Martin," said Beth.

"He should, Beth. And he was drinking?"

"Yes, Dad. I think he was already drunk."

Michaela left the room, sensing her parents wanted to work through this new information alone.

"We raised her right, Martin."

"Yeah, because your parents raised you right, and my parents did the same thing. And now one of our parents has gone astray, and I don't know what to do."

"You could pick up the phone. Or visit."

"Yeah, I could. But what good would it do? He behaved like a fool in front of his granddaughter—the granddaughter he could have killed. He certainly doesn't want to see me or any of us."

They stared at each other, hoping the other would land upon a brilliant solution.

"We let it play out, then?" asked Beth.

"I think that's what I'm saying, yes. But what if—"

"What if we get a visit from the police in two days telling us they found him unresponsive after the neighbors called because they were concerned the newspapers were accumulating in his driveway?"

"Yeah, that." Martin chuckled at the detailed nature of his wife's description.

"It's not exactly funny, dear, but—"

"Yeah, I know you're not 'laughing' laughing," said Beth. "But there isn't much we can do. He's an adult."

"But it can't end with the police knocking on our door at 3:00 a.m. His story deserves a way better resolution, despite what he's put us through."

Beth grabbed her husband's hand.

"Dear God, please reach that stubborn man. Please let him know it's not too late. Please make him aware how much we love him and that we desperately want and need him to be the man he was."

"Amen," whispered Martin.

The second Michaela pulled out of his driveway, Franklin felt waves of shame wash over him. He felt even worse than he did on the Fourth. She would never forgive him now. None of them would. What else could he do but have a few more drinks, fall asleep on the floor, and awaken to a new, horrible day?

"Oh, Ruth," he called out, "I shunned our granddaughter. I hurt our granddaughter. She came to help, and I played the fool again. What have I done? What have I become?"

"Is it time for another adventure, pal?" asked Red.

"What are you talking about?"

"You know, like we did a few months ago—a return to nature."

"Red, I'll admit that it was fun, but we got lucky. Maybe next time, we don't get so lucky."

"Fatty, focus on the first part of your thought. It was fun. You know it. And this time, Mom can join us."

"Red, you're not making any sense. Why would Mom want to join us outside?"

"No, not Mama—Mom. You know, Aurora."

"That's a bad idea. Why drag her into this? She belongs to other humans."

"Just answer me this, Fatty. Does at least a part of you want to go outside?"

"Sure, Red, but—"

"Bup-bup-bup. Focus on that part. Now, did anything go wrong the first time? Mama and Papa still have no idea we escaped and returned."

"No, Red, nothing went wrong the first time, but—"

"Again, Fatty, I need to bup-bup-bup you. So, let's review. We had fun. Nothing bad happened. The only question I have is this: Why wouldn't we want to do it again?"

"Because, Red, this time maybe something goes wrong, and our humans would be worried sick about us. And you want to bring your mom into it, too? Now let me ask you a question. If you asked Mom or Kind Sir to let us out for a bit to roam the neighborhood, what do you think their answer would be?"

"They'd say no, Fatty. Duh. That's why we have to do it without them knowing!"

Fatty sighed.

"Isn't that a strong indication that we shouldn't be planning a second trip, bud?"

Red had to admit that Fatty had a point. But he persisted.

"But be honest. You wouldn't mind occasionally being outside, right? I mean, you had it rough out there, but now it's different. You take a little outdoor trip, sniff a few things, chase a mouse, but you know you have a safe place to return to."

"Yes, Red, you're right. But what you're planning is dangerous and sneaky and—"

"Let's talk to the boy. He helped us the first time."

"Oh, that's right. We could've gotten Luca in trouble, too."

"Fatty, let's go have a chat with him. It can't hurt."

So, they ambled into Luca's room. He put down his guitar when he sensed they were on some sort of mission.

"What are you guys up to?"

"Remember when you helped us escape a few months back?" asked Red.

"Yeah. What about it?"

"Well, if we ever wanted to do it again, do you think you'd help us?"

"We all got lucky the first time. Do you have any idea how much trouble we'd be in if something happened? Let's not press our luck, Red."

"See, Red? Luca gets it."

"Oh, you two. Again, nothing happened the first time. You know why? Because we're cats. We're fast. We're sleek. We don't get in trouble."

"Well, Fatty isn't exactly sleek," said Luca. "No offense, pal."

"None taken, Luca."

"Yeah, true. But she's fast. You've seen her play. She's got great reflexes. And, Fatty, you survived by your wits for a long time outside. Do you really think something bad is going to happen if we sneak away for an hour?"

"Yeah, that is a good point."

Red was starting to win his friend over, and Luca wanted to get back to his guitar and knew agreeing with Red on some future mission was the quickest way to achieve this.

"Then it's agreed. The next time an opportunity arises for us to sneak out, you'll help us."

"Red, I've agreed to nothing," said Fatty.

"And sure, if you have some foolproof plan, Red, I'll consider helping you," said Luca.

Red heard what he wanted to hear. "As I said, it's agreed."

"Goodbye, you two," said Luca as he started strumming louder.

"When the stars align, friend, it's 'Outdoors: The Sequel.'"

Fatty said nothing, letting her nose lead the way into the kitchen, where someone was most definitely cooking seafood.

Though he and Beth had agreed to let the situation with Franklin play out, it was gnawing at Martin, and, following the path of his daughter, he decided to pay a visit to the old man to see if he could make things better. Apparently, he wasn't as stubborn as his father.

He knocked, but there was no response. So, he sat on the porch rocker and figured Franklin would relent at some point.

Minutes passed. No sign of Franklin. Martin expected as much, and while he feared his wife's narrative may have come to reality, he figured it was mere stubbornness that was keeping his father inside.

Martin was prepared. He walked to his car, popped the trunk, and withdrew a basketball. What was left of the hoop in the driveway was frayed, but all he needed was a rim. Shooting hoops with his sisters and friends provided hours of entertainment in their youth. And he could remember like it was yesterday the first time he beat his dad one-on-one. He was certain this would draw his father out of the house.

At first, Franklin assumed the bouncing basketball was coming from neighborhood kids. Then he realized it was a bit closer. He shuffled upstairs and saw his son shooting jumpers. Martin was still wearing a tie and suit slacks. The sight of a 50-year-old man dressed for work but playing a game to get his father's attention forced Franklin to react.

Martin had been playing for at least ten minutes now. Not exactly dressed for the occasion, he was missing way more than he made. Neighbors were no doubt viewing the spectacle. For all he knew, some were even recording on their phones. He feared going viral on YouTube, under a headline such as "Middle-Aged Man Doing LeBron Impersonation, Failing Spectacularly."

"Come on, old man," he thought. "Get down here. I don't have much left in the tank."

Finally, the garage door opened.

"Go home, Martin. Leave me be."

"No, Dad." He approached his father. "Gah, you reek of whiskey."

"And you reek of desperation. And your jumper needs work."

"This isn't a joking matter, Dad. Michaela came here out of the goodness of her hear—"

"And I'll tell you what I told her: Go home. Now, preferably."

Martin was flummoxed and unsure of how to proceed. So, he did nothing. He figured he'd stand his ground and see how his father would react.

Franklin shrugged and went back in the house.

So, Martin did what any man in such a circumstance would do: He picked up the orange sphere and threw it as hard as he humanly could against the garage door, leaving a basketball-shaped imprint. If somebody were filming, at least Martin would provide a memorable closing scene.

"Did you walk home, honey?" asked Beth, upon seeing the condition of her suit-wearing, basketball-playing husband.

"No, I'm hot . . . and I'm also hot," said Martin.

He was pacing around the kitchen while untying his tie. Beth had a million questions but held her tongue, figuring it was best to let her husband explain.

"That man—ugh! I went over there, all right? Yeah, I know what we agreed to the other day, but what you said stuck in my head. It can't end like that. It just can't, Beth."

Martin's voice was breaking, but he continued.

"I tossed the basketball in the trunk before I left for work this morning. I figured it'd draw him out. I was playing for heaven knows how long, looking like an idiot, probably putting on a show for the old neighborhood. And he finally emerged."

"Was he drunk?" asked Beth.

"Yeah. And rude, just like he was to Michaela. He told me to go home. I stared at him, hoping he might break. He didn't."

"And so, it played out the same as Michaela's attempt to reach him."

"Yeah, but with one small difference." Martin chuckled.

"Why don't I like that chuckle?"

"Before I left, I hurled the basketball as hard as I could at his garage door."

"You didn't."

"Oh, believe me. I did." He chuckled again.

"Did it make you feel better?"

"It did! But I realize that in addition to having a drunk, stubborn father whose condition seems to be worsening, I now owe the old fool a new garage door."

"You always taught us that angry throwing is wrong and will lead to more problems, Dad," said Michaela.

"There are exceptions to every rule, dear. And where did you come from, anyway? And how long have you been eavesdropping?"

"I just got home, and I caught only the last part of your story. But I'm assuming it's Grandpa who invoked your rage. Unless, of course, you're throwing basketballs at your coworkers."

"No, that kind of behavior is frowned upon at the office. And yes, it was Grandpa's innocent garage door that was in the wrong place at the wrong time, just standing there, with a bored look on its face, waiting to be pummeled."

"Well, Mom, it's either your or Dylan's turn next to get the angry, drunken Grandpa treatment. Dad and I tried and failed miserably, and now there's a shattered garage door calling its lawyer and getting fitted for a neck brace as we sit here and plan what to do next."

Beth put her arms around her daughter's shoulders.

"We do nothing, dear, because there's nothing we can do. Your father and I agreed to as much the other night, but he loves his father dearly and just couldn't resist giving it one more shot."

"So, now what? We wait?" asked Michaela.

Both Martin and Beth shrugged, lacking a better response.

INEVITABLY, SUMMER TURNS TO fall and with it came a big change to Luca's life: the beginning of middle school. His last year of elementary school certainly had its share of surprises, but Red's show put an end to Luca being shunned by his friends. He had mended fences with Jonathan and all of his pals, and he was looking forward to a new school and interesting adventures.

The whole family gathered by the front door to give Luca a proper send-off on his first day.

"Remember, Luca. The cats don't talk," said Vic.

"Papa, your disinformation campaign is equal parts outrageous and hurtful," said Red.

"You know what he means, smart guy," said Claudia.

"You just want to put on another performance, don't you, Red?" said Fatty. "Admit it."

"No!" said Red, perhaps a touch too defensively.

"All right, champ, have a great first day, and don't think about these knuckleheads," said Claudia.

"I will, Mom, and I won't, Mom," said Luca.

The cats were momentarily displeased at being referred to as "knuckleheads," but they knew Claudia meant no harm, and they both head-butted Luca on his legs as he departed.

"'Knucklehead' can be a term of endearment, you two, in case you were wondering," said Claudia.

They both kept staring at Claudia.

"No, really, guys, she's telling the truth," said Vic.

"Got it, jerkface," said Red.

"Yeah, no, that's not the same thing, pal," said Vic.

Fatty tried stifling a giggle.

"Hey, guys, since Luca's not here, I want to tell you what he wants for Christmas," said Fatty.

"Should we be scared?" asked Claudia.

"I don't know, but it's called a Fender Strato—something."

"Stratocaster," said Vic.

"Yeah, that's it! Red and white," said Fatty.

"Ah, you can never go wrong with red," said Red.

"Well, we'll take it under consideration, Fatty. Thanks for letting us know. How did you find out, anyway?" asked Claudia.

"That night you took Red to meet his mom. We had a chat while he was practicing."

"Ah, I see," said Vic. "And what do you guys want, since you brought up the subject?"

"We get Christmas presents, too?" asked Red.

"Well, sure, assuming you behave," said Claudia.

"Why are you looking just at me?" asked Red.

Fatty was giving Vic's gift proposal deep thought and then blurted out a single word in response.

"Prosciutto," she said.

Vic and Claudia exchanged looks.

"I'd like some prosciutto for Christmas," said Fatty.

"Oh, yeah, Fatty, that is an excellent choice. That stuff is salty and delicious. Remember you gave us some a couple months ago?" asked Red.

"I do remember that," said Vic, laughing. "That's not the answer I was expecting, but that's a simple-enough request."

"And way cheaper than a Stratocaster," said Claudia.

"So, you're saying we should shoot for something more expensive?" asked Red.

"No, Reddy MacRedson, that's not at all what I'm saying, but you do have a few months to alter or add to your request—within reason," said Claudia.

The two cats scampered out of the kitchen.

"So, now I'm Scottish, apparently," said Red.

"Perhaps someone can knit you a kilt," said Fatty.

Red thought about this for a moment, imagining himself in red tartan.

"I'd look awesome in a kilt, Fatty."

"Is there anything you wouldn't look awesome in, Red?"

"I know you're trying to mock me, friend, but if I'm being honest, the answer is no. And to complete the ensemble, Fatty, I have one word for you: tam-o'-shanter."

"You're hopeless, Red."

"That's Reddy MacRedson. And you're just jealous, mate."

"So, do we put a red bow on a pound of lunch meat, or do we stuff it in a stocking? What's the protocol on that?" asked Vic.

"Did you see how earnest Fatty's face was? She really gave it some thought. She's so adorable," said Claudia.

"We should tell Luca to make them something out of cardboard for Christmas."

"That's a great idea, Vic. And what do you want Santa to bring, since we're discussing Christmas?"

"Hmm . . . I'm going to follow the cats' lead and say a pound of fettucine."

Claudia chuckled. "Well, I'm off to work, dear."

"Yep, me too. That Stratocaster isn't going to just show up like magic on our doorstep, is it?"

VIC WAS STUMPED ON a project he was working on, so he grabbed his phone and went searching for the cats.

They were both sitting on the landing windowsill, staring outside and, in a rare moment, being regular cats.

"All right, you two. I have questions, and you can supply the answers."

"Bored at work, Papa?" asked Red.

"No, I just need a creative jolt, and I figure you two might be able to supply it."

"Okay, ask away. You know I love to talk."

Vic: Okay, so, what's the deal with heights? Why do you love them so much?

Red: It's easier to survey the fields. Duh!

Vic: Yeah, I understand that's why wild cats do it. But this is a home, not the savannah. A gazelle isn't going to come traipsing through the living room.

Red: But if one were to, Papa, boom, I'm on it. If someone had said to you a few months ago you'd be having a conversation with a cat, would you have believed them? I rest my case.

Vic: Yeah, I suppose you do make a point. From now on, you're on gazelle duty, Red.

Red saluted.

Vic: What about you, Fatty? Leaping isn't exactly your thing, is it?

Fatty: No.

Red: Yeah, but she makes up for it with her super-fast paw.

Fatty: It's true. I had to survive out there somehow.

Vic: And did you have a favorite dinner?

Fatty: Just the usual—rodents and birds, sometimes the occasional—

Red: Wait. You ate animals out there?

Fatty: Of course, Red. What did you think I did, order pizza?

Red: Well, yeah. Did you ever think of doing that? It would have been a lot less bloody and murder-y.

Fatty: You realize you eat animals every day, too, right? Just because our food's in a can doesn't make it any different than what outside cats do.

Red: I guess that never occurred to me. Still, it's different somehow. You're a killing machine.

Vic: Red, she had to survive out there. Anyway, Fatty, before you were interrupted, you were saying "and the occasional . . ."

Fatty: Rabbit.

Red: Bunnies?! You killed cute, little bunny rabbits?

Fatty: Not all the time, Red, though I have to admit they are pretty tasty.

Red scooched closer to Vic.

Red: Papa, can I sleep between you and Mama tonight? I'd feel a lot safer.

Vic: Red, you're being ridiculous. Fatty had to survive in nature. She had no choice.

Red: There's fields and fields of grass. You could have been a yard-etarian, chum.

Fatty: Cats can't survive by eating grass.

Red: How about people's garbage?

Fatty: Sure. I did that all the time. But the best parts were things like chicken wings with some meat left on the bones.

Vic: So, Red, can we fix you a big salad for dinner, then? Some nice lettuce, tomatoes, onions?

Red: I'm not hungry. And I'm not sleeping ever again. I just found out my best pal is a homicidal maniac. How would you like it if you found out Mama used to be a hunter?

Vic: Claudia used to go hunting with her father all the time when she was young, Reddy.

Red: I'm sleeping in Luca's room tonight and forever. With the door locked. I trust no one.

Fatty snuck up behind Red and nibbled his ear.

Red: Aah!

Fatty and Vic couldn't stop laughing.

Red: There's nothing funny about that. And now I've thought of a brand-new reason I like heights. You can't eat me if you can't reach me.

Fatty: No one's going to eat you, Red. You're way too skinny.

Vic: All right, you two. I think you've recharged my battery. Back to the salt mines.

Red: Papa, can I sit in your office today? I don't want to be alone with you-know-who.

Fatty: Red, you're being ridiculous.

Vic: Yes, Red, Fatty's right. You are being ridiculous. Run along, you two, and thanks for the interview.

Vic chuckled his way back to the office and shut the door behind him.

Red and Fatty headed to the living room, with Red keeping a few feet of distance between them.

"Seriously, Red?" asked Fatty.

"What? I'm just walking, same as you, pal."

"Yes, but I'm literally having to raise my voice for you to hear me because you keep drifting away." She giggled. "You're afraid of me, aren't you?"

"What?! I'm not afraid of anything." He scooched closer to show her he wasn't scared.

"Okay, Red. I believe you. But did I ever tell you about the time I felled a horse and devoured it in a single sitting?"

Pshoo! Red was atop the bookcase in a flash, and Fatty was literally rolling on the ground guffawing.

Realizing she was telling a tall tale, Red gently descended the shelf and rejoined his friend as nonchalantly as he could.

"That wasn't funny, Fatty."

"Yeah, it totally was, you goof."

"I'm still keeping an eye on you."

Fatty bared her fangs. Red jumped to his right.

Fatty was starting to feel bad about teasing her friend, and she knew what subject would get him to stop being jumpy. "Let's talk about our next adventure."

"Really? Sweet. Let's sneak off to the boy's room. We don't want Papa to hear us."

It was a new school for Luca, and the old problems had all but disappeared. The only time anyone mentioned the talking-cat incident was to praise Red's performance and how awesome it was. The seventh grade was progressing well for Luca, and before anyone knew it, Halloween was around the corner.

And while Luca and his friends were debating the pros and cons of various costumes—Spider-Man? A Minecraft character?—Franklin Betters was preparing for the worst night of the year.

For every football and Frisbee he confiscated during the year, Halloween was payback night.

And even though he closed every blind and shut off every light, they knew he was there, and as soon as the sun set, the serenading would commence.

Sung to the familiar arena chant of "Let's go (home team)/clap-clap, clap-clap-clap," the neighborhood kids would belt out "Old Man Bitters" but instead of clapping, every clap was replaced with a perfectly timed egg splattering against the old drunk's house.

And then they would laugh, and there was nothing he could do about it. If he dared open his door and set foot on his porch, the boys wouldn't have hesitated for a second to pelt him with eggs.

So, he cowered in darkness until the kids ran out of eggs, the whiskey doing its best to dim his anger, or at least get him to sleep quicker.

What's funny is that back in the day, in the happier portion of his life, Franklin and Ruth loved the holiday as much as their children did, and their home on Halloween was decked out like no one else's in the neighborhood. Bats hanging from the windows. Big jack-o'-lanterns adorning the porch. Strings of pumpkin lights draped over the bushes. And the Betterses? Their house was the most popular destination on all the trick-or-treaters' itineraries because they handed out full-size candy bars.

And now? "Old Man Bitters"/egg-egg, egg-egg-egg.

Martin and Beth exchanged nervous glances between handing out candy to the various ghosts and Batmen who showed up on their doorstep.

"You want to go, don't you?"

Martin sighed. "Of course I do. You know what's happening over there."

"Trick or treat!"

"Oh, wow! A unicorn and an Incredible Hulk. You guys look great!"

"Thank you!"

"Yeah, I know, but he's probably passed out and unaware of what's going on."

"And that's supposed to calm me, Beth?"

"Trick or treat!"

"Huh! It's Troy Polamalu and Harry Potter! Awesome, dudes!"

"Thank you."

"No, it's not meant to calm you. It's meant to help you see the truth."

"Trick or treat!"

"But if I can shoo the kids away and make his night a little less awful, I should do what I can, no?"

Buzz Lightyear and Woody stood there, not sure what to do as the adults were working out their issue.

"Oh, yeah, you guys look great. Here you go."

"Thank you."

"Martin, honey, go. I think I can handle Kit Kat duty by myself."

Martin hopped in his car and made the short trip to his father's house in twice the time it would normally take because the streets were filled with princesses and zombies and space aliens focused on their haul and little distracted by a middled-aged man trying to make a bad situation slightly less dire.

When he finally arrived, his worst fears were confirmed: a group of teenage boys, not even bothering to wear costumes, were laughing hysterically as they pelted the house he grew up in with egg after egg.

"Stop it, you guys. That's enough. Go home."

"Or what, old man?" yelled one.

"Yeah, what are you gonna do about it?" yelled another, to the delight of the rest.

Martin pulled out his cellphone. "Throw one more egg, and I call the cops. Now go home."

The boy who first spoke grabbed another egg and cocked his arm.

"I've dialed the 9 and the first 1."

The boy snarled at Martin but made the decision that following through with his throw probably wasn't worth a visit from the police and a parental grounding. He turned tail, and his poseur posse followed suit.

A few of the kids actually lived in the neighborhood, and Martin rolled his eyes as he saw them enter their homes. "They don't realize I could still call the cops on them for what they did here, do they?" Martin said to himself.

"They're not the brightest bulbs on the street."

Martin jumped, having no clue where the voice was coming from.

"Oh, I'm sorry, Martin. I didn't mean to startle you."

"Mrs. Garetti. I didn't see you standing there."

She chuckled. "Well, it's Halloween, isn't it? Boo!"

Martin looked at the teens' handiwork and sighed.

"Well, I better hose these off now. It'll only be worse in the morning."

"You're a good son, Martin."

"Well, I try, but—"

"Martin, I've lived here for more than 50 years. I've seen you and your siblings grow up. I remember Ruth, and I know the situation with your father. Of course, it's absolutely none of my business, but if I can ever be of help . . ."

"And you've always been a wonderful neighbor. Actually, you can help. My father has shut us out. He doesn't want to talk to us. We fear the worst. If you ever see anything amiss, please give us a call."

"Of course. It's the least I can do. Um, I hope I'm not prying, but what exactly happened to the garage door?"

Martin chuckled. "Ah, that was a souvenir from my visit a little while back. Let's just say it didn't go as planned."

"We elderly parents can bring out the worst in you whippersnappers, eh?"

"You have no idea, Mrs. Garetti, and I'm not half the whippersnapper I used to be."

The two exchanged smiles, and Martin got to work cleaning the exterior of his father's house.

Meanwhile, a few blocks away, Luca and Jonathan—or for one night a Dementor and Voldemort—were planning the smartest route for the greatest haul.

"No, dude, we cut through the cul-de-sac and skip a chunk of Freeport Road, because most of the houses there are dark, anyway," said Luca.

And as they debated, in walked Red and Fatty, decked out for the holiday and on strict orders to be regular cats for the evening.

Fatty looked regal in her pink Cinderella gown, while Reddy Mac-Redson was adorned in a red tartan kilt and sporting a red tam-o'-shanter.

"Bro, your cats are the best," said Jonathan, still amazed by Red's school performance the previous year.

The family held its collective breath as Red jumped right on Jonathan's lap.

"That hat is awesome, dude!"

Red wanted to say, "It's called a tam-o'-shanter, and my name's not 'dude,'" but he held his tongue, much to everyone's relief, and gave Jonathan a good-natured head-butt.

"All right, you two," said Claudia, knowing her showman of a cat could remain silent for only so long, "hit the road. Mama needs some free peanut-butter cups."

"Not a chance, Mom!" said Luca, as he and Jonathan departed.

Every trick-or-treater and accompanying parent enjoyed the show that Red and Fatty put on. The parents marveled that the cats were keeping on their outfits, and the kids chuckled at Red's various jumping antics. They were a hit.

"I wish Halloween were every month, Mama," said Red when there was a lull in the activity. "This is awesome."

"Yeah, but you two don't have a sweet tooth like us humans do. If Halloween were every month, your father and I wouldn't fit through the doorway."

"But can we maybe dress up on holidays?" asked Fatty.

"Of course, Fatty! You look lovely, by the way."

"Thanks, Mom."

After a few hours, Jonathan and Luca returned and dumped their dentists' nightmare on the living-room floor and bartered for the next 20 minutes, with Jonathan gladly accepting gummy bears and the like for the chocolate that Luca loved best.

Vic and Claudia jokingly distracted Luca and snuck off with a Twix and a few Snickers bars.

The cats kept their outfits on till bedtime, looking forward to Thanksgiving and what they might wear next.

And, after a few hours, Martin finally got the last of the egg residue off the bricks. His father wouldn't be aware of what Martin did till morning, when the old man retrieved the paper from the driveway. He would be touched by what his son did, but he was still too stubborn to pick up the phone, and he was still mad at the world.

MARTIN SAT IN THE living room, staring at his cellphone. It was three days before Thanksgiving.

"You know," Beth said, "someone famous once said, 'Do or do not. There is no try.'"

Martin frowned, then chuckled.

"Well, dear, what do you think I should do . . . or do not?"

"I have no idea. But you've been sighing to yourself all week. Your wheels have been turning so much, it's a wonder you're not standing in California."

"Okay, best-case scenario: I call him, and not only does he accept, but he's sober and apologetic. He comes to our house Thursday—dapper, sociable, witty, the best version of himself. We all have a wonderful day, and the kids get to meet their real grandfather for the first time."

"And worst-case scenario?"

"He says yes but is half in the tank by the time he gets here. He behaves like a clown, and, I don't know, there's an incident in the kitchen with the turkey, and this time Dylan gets set ablaze. The house explodes, cartoon-like, and we're all holding individual 'Help' signs as we land in various neighbors' yards."

"You really think that's a realistic outcome?"

"Well, maybe not the cartoon part, but the rest? There's a chance."

"He might say no, assuming he answers his phone."

"Yeah, there's that, too. That would provide a sense of relief . . . but also of guilt. And if he does say yes, I have to make sure to not screw up like I did on the Fourth, by reminding him to behave. So, then, I'm forced to accept his behavior, for fear of setting off another catastrophe."

Beth sighed. "Call him. Now. At least you'll have your answer, and we can go from there."

Martin punched in the number and held his breath.

"Hello?"

"Dad? Hey, it's Martin. We were wondering if you'd like to join us on Thursday. Everyone will be here."

"Am I on strict orders to behave?"

"Well, that would be ni—it would be nice if you came. We'd all like to see you."

"Fine. See you Thursday."

Click.

Martin looked up at his wife.

"That was fast. Well?"

"He's coming. He asked me if he was on 'strict orders to behave.'"

"Ah, we're getting off on the right foot, then, eh?"

"Yeah, well, at least he's coming, and at least that's off my mind. You were right, Beth. I do feel better. Now all I have to worry about is Thursday."

"See, honey? One fewer thing to worry about. That's half the battle sometimes."

"In case I haven't told you lately, I'm glad I said 'I do.'"

"Yeah, saying 'I do not' would have made for a really ugly ceremony. And what would we have done about the reception?"

"Oh, you have the reception regardless. The hall's paid for. The food and drinks are ordered. You just skip the bridal dance."

"Who's getting married?" asked Dylan as he entered the room.

"Uh, no one. We were just speculating about what couples do when they say 'I do not.' Anyway, good news. Your grandfather's joining us for Thanksgiving."

Dylan looked at his father, unsure of what to say.

"Okay, I get it, slugger. Perhaps not good news, but news that makes your father potentially happy. So, there's that."

"If you say so, Dad. I hope there isn't a scene."

He grabbed a Gatorade from the fridge and went back upstairs.

"My father's going to be a punchline to the kids. Every time they get together in the future, one of them will inevitably say, 'Hey, remember the time Grandpa . . .' and the ending of that setup will never be pretty."

"Like 'You remember the time Grandpa almost killed you on the Fourth?'"

"Dang it, Beth. Tell me there's still time for better memories."

"There is, Martin. But there's nothing we can do. It's all up to the old man."

And the old man knew exactly how he was going to behave on Thanksgiving.

JESSICA WAS THE FIRST to arrive.

"Hey!" said Martin, as he gave his younger sister a hug.

"Look at you guys. I'm glad you could make it."

"Are we early?" asked her husband.

"No! Someone has to be first, right? Come on in. Of course . . ."

"I don't like that pause, Martin."

"Well, someone has to pick up Dad, and since you got here first . . ."

"Fine. I'll go. Any indication on what I'm walking into?"

"Nope. I invited him on Monday, he surprisingly said yes, and I haven't spoken to him since."

"Good luck, Jess!" yelled Beth from the kitchen.

"Uh, yeah, thanks, sis-in-law. I thought the warmth was coming from the oven, but clearly it's your heart that's overwhelming me."

Jessica shrugged. "Fine. Be back in a half-hour. Wish me luck."

When she reached her father's house, he was waiting for her on the front porch. He appeared to be sober. So far, so good.

"You drew the short straw, huh?" Franklin said to her as she pulled up.

Not wanting to add tension to what promised to be a stressful day, she didn't respond.

"Hello, Dad. Hey, what happened to your garage door?"

"Oh, that? You'd have to ask St. Martin about it."

Jessica regretted asking the question, seeing how it was clearly a sore spot and another potential Thanksgiving land mine.

The entirety of the trip was safe and silent, except for brief exchanges about an early winter and the Steelers' playoff hopes.

"Hey, we're back," said Jessica, trying to be cheerful but fearing the worst.

Martin's greeting to his father was met with a terse nod.

"Well, everyone's in the living room, so come on in."

Everyone greeted Franklin warmly, which again he acknowledged with a quick nod. The lively conversations came to a sudden stop, with everyone wondering what Franklin was up to.

Finally, he spoke.

"So, St. Martin, are you putting me at the kiddies' table today in case I misbehave?"

"Dad, it's incredibly difficult for a child—even one as gray-haired as I am—to chide a parent, but apparently you're leaving me no choice. Everyone in this room loves you, and we invited you because we want you to be with us. Now, my wife has worked hard for days preparing a lovely holiday meal. I'd rather you not ruin it."

"Well, by the smell of it, that ship's already sailed, son."

But before Martin could lay into his father for his childish insult, in walked Beth, laughing.

"Oh, Franklin, you always were a quick wit," she said, planting a good-natured kiss on his forehead.

The family headed into the dining room, nervously chuckling over Beth's retort, admiring her for helping them all dodge the first volley but fully aware that the fusillade had just begun.

Inevitably, the discussions turned to the weather and sports, harmless subjects in which they agreed, and Franklin sat and ate in silence, until it was Jane's turn to feel his wrath.

"So, Jane," he began, "still not married, huh? How come?"

"Well, Dad, it's not really your business, is it?" she said.

"No, of course not. If you've decided to become an old maid, that's entirely your choice."

"Dad, that's enough," said Martin.

"That's enough what, St. Martin? Would you like me to go home?"

"No, of course not. But the only thing you've done is attack us since you arrived. And you know what? You can lay off the 'St. Martin' nonsense, too."

Everyone stopped eating.

"You owe me $1,432.50," said Franklin.

"What on Earth for, Dad?"

"A new garage door. Why don't you tell everyone what happened to it? I'm sure they'd love to hear."

"Okay, and, Dad, after I do that, maybe you can ask my daughter how her arm is. How about that?"

"Franklin, Martin, let's not—"

"No, Beth, it's okay. I'll tell everyone about the garage door."

The labors of Beth's kitchen skills were going cold before everyone's eyes.

"A few months ago, after what happened on the Fourth, I decided to pay him a visit. I tossed a basketball in the trunk, thinking I could entice the old man out of hiding. It worked . . . sort of. We had a brief, angry exchange, and the situation made me so furious that for a moment I lost my temper and threw the ball as hard as I could at his garage door."

"And the garage-door man said it's unfixable. A new one'll cost you almost $1,500."

Franklin proceeded to eat.

"Are you for real, old man?"

"Martin, honey, he's trying his best to get—"

"Under my skin, Beth. Yeah, I get it. Fine, Dad. You win. But before you leave—and you will be leaving very shortly—I want you to apologize to Michaela. Do it. Now!"

Franklin placed his fork gently on his plate and said, "It was an accident. What you did to my garage door was nothing of the sort." He picked up his fork and resumed eating.

Pointing to Michaela, Martin said, "You're comparing my daughter—your granddaughter!—to a sheet of metal?!" Spit flew from his mouth as he was saying this. No one had ever seen him madder. There was a good chance the neighbors heard every word.

"That young lady has a good heart, Dad. You know what she did?" he said, looking at everyone but his father. "She visited the old drunk after the accident. Yeah. She visited him. She was the one who reached out. And he was rude to her."

Franklin helped himself to some more mashed potatoes. "I'll take that check and be on my way."

Everyone froze, not knowing where the next volley was going to come from.

"Oh, and, Beth? These potatoes need more salt."

Martin threw his napkin on his seat, went upstairs, and emerged a moment later brandishing his checkbook. He wrote out the check with such rage that surely the next five checks would be rendered useless, bearing the imprint of "One-thousand, four-hundred, thirty-two and 50/100."

He tore the check at the perforation and all but threw it in Franklin's direction.

"Jess, would you do us a favor and take our father home," said Martin, "seeing how you're one of the few adults he didn't insult today?"

"Sure, Martin. Come on, Dad. I'm sure you can hurl some invective my way on the trip home."

Franklin folded the check, put it in his shirt pocket, and departed with his older daughter.

Everyone sat in silence until Martin spoke.

"You know what's ironic?"

"Uh . . . you need a drink?" asked Beth.

"Bingo!"

Everyone chuckled.

"I need a beer. In fact, Beth, find as many beers as you can in the fridge, open them all, pour them in an aquarium, and get me a straw."

"Okay, dear, but first, do you think you could help me reheat everything?"

"Yes, absolutely." He exhaled. "The people I love most are all in this room. We are blessed to be together. We'll resume worrying about the old man tomorrow. But let's enjoy the rest of the day."

Everyone raised a glass.

"Do you want to talk, Dad?" asked Jessica. "I mean, this isn't you."

"I'm sober, aren't I?"

"What, so those are the choices we have—drunk and prone to starting fires or sober but vicious?"

"Or you can all leave me alone. There's a third choice for you."

"Then why did you accept Martin's invitation?"

"I wanted to collect for the garage-door damage."

"You have the money for a new gar—" Jessica sighed. "None of this makes sense. None of it!"

"Just leave me alone—all of you."

"You're making that a real possibility, Dad."

Not a word was spoken the rest of the way. Finally alone, Franklin took a satisfying swig directly from the whiskey bottle, sat in his favorite recliner, and wept into his hands.

Jessica returned to her waiting family, and they all put on their best faces and tried their best to have a happy holiday, ignoring the fresh scene Franklin provided for them, and focusing on each other's company.

When the siblings found themselves alone in the kitchen, however, Martin grabbed both his sisters in a bear hug and, fighting back tears, said, "I don't know him anymore. And, even worse, I'm not sure I want to know him."

The three of them consoled each other until Jessica looked directly at Jane and said, "Really, though, why aren't you married?"

They couldn't stop laughing, proving once again that laughter and tears aren't quite the opposites we all assume they are.

"Why the dirty look, Red? We brought you leftover turkey," said Vic.

"Well, yeah, but we were alone on a holiday. That's unforgivable."

"We go to my brother's house for Thanksgiving. They'll be here for Christmas. That's the way it works. Besides, did you and Fatty not enjoy your pilgrim outfits?"

"Yes. Yes, we did. But we didn't get to show them off to anybody else."

"And you and Fatty don't seem to mind the turkey, either."

"It's delicious, Kind Sir. Red, if you don't want yours . . ."

"I said no such thing, friend. Hush."

The two resumed eating their leftover holiday feast.

"Honey, Lisa's coming over around 1:00 to drop off the cat. We'll probably be gone most of the day."

"That's fine, Claud. I'm hanging out with Keith to watch some football, which means," Vic said, looking at Luca, "you'll be in charge of three cats. Think you can handle it?"

"No problem, Dad."

Red shot Fatty a look, but she was too involved in her turkey to notice.

Later, when they were alone, Red reminded Fatty of her promise from a while back.

"It's the perfect setup," said Red. "It'll be just like last time. What could go wrong?"

"Everything!" said Fatty. "Let's not press our luck."

"It's a beautiful day. My mom is coming over. Mama and Papa will be out of our hair all day. All we have to do is convince Luca."

"Or we could just hang out with your mom and have a nice day. Yeah, let's do that."

Red sighed.

"Fatty, do we have to go through this song-and-dance again? Tell me with a straight face you don't want to feel the grass under your paws, breathe in some nice outdoor air, and make goofy faces to the various pets we'll encounter."

"Yes, Red, that all sounds enticing, but—"

Red said nothing and let Fatty's "but" hang in the air.

She furrowed her brow and said, "Okay, fine. Yes, I want to go. How do we convince Luca? And what about your mom?"

"I'm sure my mother misses being outside, too. And Luca? It's easier this time. He can let us out the front door and then let us back in."

That afternoon, Lisa and Claudia were Black Friday shopping, Keith and Vic were watching football, and the three cats found themselves staring up at Luca, who was deeply involved in a game of Angry Birds.

"What do you guys want?" he finally asked.

"The grass beneath our paws, bro," said Red.

It took a second for Luca to grasp Red's request.

"I don't know, guys. You got lucky last time. Mom and Dad left in me charge today. If anything happens—"

"Bro, what could happen? Last time involved cracked-open windows and roofs. This time? You open the door, let us out, and you can return to your exploding-pig game in no time."

"Promise me you'll be back in half an hour?"

"Absolutely."

Luca figured there would be no harm. These weren't regular cats, after all. They were smart enough to avoid danger. Plus, he wouldn't mind practicing his guitar by himself for a change. He relented.

"All right, you guys. Be back in a half-hour!" said Luca as the cats sprinted out the front door.

"Isn't this great, Mom?"

Aurora was getting adjusted to the feeling of the grass. She hadn't been outside since before she wound up at the shelter. She was almost overwhelmed.

It was an unseasonably warm November day. The grass wasn't yet snow-covered. The birds were chirping. The three of them were rolling on the ground, laughing, and having a wonderful time.

They came to a fenced-in yard where they found a sleeping beagle.

"Let's scare him!" said Red.

"No, Red, that's not nice," said Fatty.

"But he's a doggo, our natural enemy."

"They are not our enemies, Red," said Fatty. "Most doggos are nice. I knew a bunch of them when I lived outside. Here, watch."

Red and Aurora gave Fatty the boost she needed to hop over the fence.

The beagle was at first perplexed to see an approaching cat, but as soon as Fatty nuzzled his head, the beagle let out a happy, little yelp and acted like he had a new best friend.

Red and Aurora then leapt the fence, and the four of them happily jumped around for a bit before the three cats resumed their adventure. They knew it was only a matter of minutes before the beagle's excited chirps would elicit human attention.

"That doggo was pretty nice, Fatty," said Red. "Maybe we could convince Mama and Papa to get one."

A bird made haste as he saw the cats approaching.

"Oh, Fatty, that reminds me. Try not to kill anything while we're out today. Did I tell you about this, Mom?"

Fatty rolled her eyes.

"Fatty seems sweet, right? But she has the heart of a killer."

"Red, honey, she had to survive outside by herself. What do you think I did before we ended up at the shelter?"

Red stopped in his tracks. "I'm surrounded by maniacs."

"Maybe you should head back home, then, and be safe," said Fatty.

"Stop spouting nonsense, friend," said Red.

The three continued on their journey, and, like the first time, they made faces at various cats napping on inside windowsills, who were never amused. Fatty pretended to chase a bird, which prompted Red to yell, which, in turn, launched Aurora into a fit of laughter. Eventually, they came upon Franklin's house again.

"Let's go in this time," said Red. "I want to see your hiding place."

"Red, that's probably a bad idea," said Fatty. "Besides, we have to get back soon. We don't want to worry Luca."

They crept closer to the house. The opening in the window well had returned. It was beckoning.

"I have to admit, though," she continued, "that I do wonder what the old fool is up to. Still—"

And before she could finish her admonition, Red darted in. Aurora soon followed. And Fatty sighed and joined her friends.

Not a single item had changed. Things were a little dustier, perhaps, but the basement was still the wreck that Fatty remembered. Even the rug she hid under hadn't moved an inch.

"This is depressing me, Fatty," said Red. "I'm glad you got out of here."

Red was jumping on the various pieces of furniture and sniffing various bric-a-brac when he came upon a candleholder. He quickly shoved it to the ground, where it clanked louder than any of them had expected.

"Red! We don't want to draw attention," said Fatty.

"Ah, whatever. He's probably passed out drunk upstairs, anyway. It's not like he's going to hear us."

But Franklin did hear, and while he had spent much of the day drinking and feeling sorry for himself about his latest holiday performance, he was sober enough to make his way down the steps.

Red and Aurora quickly dove under the nearest objects to hide, but Fatty, overwhelmed with bad memories of the place, froze, and, before she knew it, she was locking eyes with her old nemesis.

"Ah, so, you're back," said Franklin. "And my, what a fat thing you've become."

And before he could react, the old man found himself with a face full of angry, snarling orange cat.

"Red!" screamed Fatty, which prompted Franklin to yell and lose his balance, falling to the floor with Red attached firmly to his cheeks.

"You—you talk?!" said a bewildered Franklin.

"Red, stop it! What are you doing?" said Fatty.

"He called you fat."

"Red, my name is literally Fatty."

"Yes, but the name 'Fatty' is adorable. Calling you fat is completely out of bounds, and I will not abide it."

Red finally loosened his grip, which helped Franklin's physical state, if not his mental one. He struggled unsuccessfully to get to his feet.

He scooched back to the nearest wall, held his head in his hands, and wept. By this time, Aurora emerged and joined her friends, prompting him to yell out, "How many of you are there?!"

"Just three, Franklin," said Fatty.

"Pal, what are you doing?" asked Red.

"The gig's up here. But I have a plan. Just go with it," she whispered.

A HALF-HOUR QUICKLY TURNED into an hour. And before Luca knew it, almost 90 minutes had passed. He was beyond the point of worrying. He had no way of contacting the cats. And he knew he couldn't call or text his parents, because how would he even begin to explain the carelessness of his actions? And Aurora! She wasn't even theirs. Luca knew if the cats didn't return soon, he would be facing a roomful of angry adults. All he wanted to do was enjoy some peaceful guitar strumming with the house to himself. And now all he could do was stare at the front door and hope the three reckless cats with no concept of time would come ambling up the walkway before any adult returned.

"How—how do you know my name?" asked Franklin.

"Maybe we know a lot about you," said Fatty.

Red and Aurora exchanged concerned glances.

Franklin managed to get to his feet, stumbled over to the window, and reaffixed the piece of wood to cover up the hole. They were trapped now.

He poured himself another drink from his cellar stash.

"Is that the best idea, Franklin?" asked Fatty.

"Nope. But what does it matter at this point? You want to hear what I did yesterday?"

"You beclowned yourself at yet another family function?" asked Red.

He nodded yes.

"And what would Ruth say about that?" asked Fatty.

"Oh, my word! You even know my wife's name! What are you?!"

"We're just simple cats, Franklin."

Aurora and Red then proceeded to perform a whole series of normal cat behaviors, stretching their legs and rolling around and jumping on and off the hi-fi and various pieces of old furniture that had accumulated over the years.

"See, Franklin? We're just a couple of normal cats."

He was mystified by the spectacle, but Franklin looked into Fatty's eyes and sensed her kindness. He began to feel deep shame washing over him, not only for hobbling an innocent animal, but for committing years of unimaginably bad actions toward his family.

He held a drink in one hand and his head in the other. He was softly crying. The three cats moved closer.

Almost four hours had passed now. Luca pleaded aloud, prayed quietly, and then openly promised God he would do any number of good deeds if the next beings who walked through the front door had four legs and tails.

But, as Luca was about to realize, sometimes God says no, for the people approaching the front door lacked tails and claws and were named Claudia and Lisa, who were in mid-conversation as they entered.

"...and next time, we have to try the new Mexican place," said Lisa.

"I know! That new mayor's really done a great job bringing new—"

And like most mothers, Claudia knew instantly something was amiss.

"What's up, Luca?" she asked.

"Um, nothing. Can we talk?"

Claudia excused herself, and she and Luca went into the living rom.

"What's wrong, pal?"

"I . . . I did something stupid."

Claudia had never seen her son so distraught before. He was shaking. She was concerned. She put her arms around his shoulders.

"Buddy, whatever it is, it'll be all right. What happened?"

"The cats—they wanted out. I shouldn't have—"

"You let the cats outside?! When? Why?" She was saying this in a quiet yell, not wanting to alarm Lisa.

"They wanted to feel the grass or something. They promised me they'd be back in a half-hour."

"And you listened to them? Did they tell you where they were going?"

"No, but nothing happened the first time—"

"The first time?!" This came out as more of a traditional yell.

"Um, not my business, Claud, but is everything okay in there?" asked Lisa.

Claudia was tongue-tied. Luca clearly felt awful, and her natural inclination was to hug her son and tell him everything would be okay. But she couldn't guarantee that. Plus, there was the problem of Aurora.

"Lisa, um, Luca did something kind of dumb."

"Uh-oh. What did he do?" asked Lisa, not grasping the severity of the situation.

"He let out the cats. They said—er, they apparently motioned that they wanted out, Luca opened the door, and poof, they were gone."

"Oh, my sweet Aurora!"

"I-I'm sorry, Mrs. Robinson. I'm sorry, Mom," said Luca as he ran from the room.

"What do we do now? They could be anywhere," said Lisa.

"Let's text our hubbies. I'm sure the four of us can figure something out," said Claudia.

"It all started the morning of our big trip," said Franklin.

The cats sat in rapt attention.

"We had worked hard all our lives, and we were going to see the world. And then . . ."

"Ruth didn't wake up," said Fatty.

Franklin nodded. "And from that point, nothing was ever the same. Fruit didn't taste as sweet. The sun didn't shine as bright. I grew numb. And then . . ."

"You found the bottle," said Fatty.

"Yep. And it eased the pain. Or at least made me forget about it for a few hours. A couple belts before bed, and I could sleep better. And then, sure, why not a drink with lunch? Before I knew it . . ."

"You turned into the neighborhood meanie, hoarding Frisbees and footballs and everything else that landed in your yard?" asked Red.

Franklin shook and nodded his head simultaneously. "Yes, but no. That's not who I am."

"But it's who you've become, unkind sir," said Fatty.

"No, that's not me. It can't be," said Franklin.

"Hey, see that candleholder on the floor, old man?" asked Red.

"Uh-huh."

"That's what you broke my friend's leg with a while back. She hobbles around to this day because of you."

Franklin again looked into Fatty's eyes. He remembered what he had done. It's something the old version of himself would have been aghast at. For the first time in a long time, Franklin was going to offer a sincere apology.

"I'm so, so sorry for the pain I caused you, friend. I can't undo what I've done. All I can do is offer my heartfelt apology. Can you forgive an old fool?"

"I can," said Fatty. "But what about your children and grandchildren?"

"They've been wonderful and patient, and I spit in their faces every chance I get. Did you happen to see the garage door on your way in?"

"Yeah, we were wondering about that," said Red.

Franklin chuckled. "My son did that, and he had every right to. He reached out to me, and I spurned him. My granddaughter reached out to me. I shunned her. I was rude to her. And that was after I almost killed her by causing a fire."

The cats looked at each other and then listened intently as Franklin recounted his Fourth of July folly.

"Wow, Fatty, I guess in comparison, you got off pretty easy," said Red.

Franklin sat silently for a moment. He felt the bitterness leaching out of his pores. But he was also exhausted, and without any warning, he fell asleep where he sat.

"Guys, I think we're here for the night," said Red.

"Our humans must be terrified," said Fatty. "And poor Luca."

"Gosh, you're right, Fatty. Why do we have a habit of getting him in trouble?"

"If we don't get out of here soon, I think Santa Cat might be giving that Fender to some other child," said Fatty.

Aurora was looking around the house as Red and Fatty chatted.

"Guys, I think we're stuck here till morning," she said.

The three of them were concerned, but they were still cats. So, they made the best of the situation and snuggled around Franklin. They would all confront their various problems after the sun returned.

KEITH AND VIC REACHED the house as soon as they could.

"Where's Luca?" asked Vic.

"He's upstairs. He's a mess," said Claudia.

"Yeah, I figured," said Vic. "Listen. Give me a sec to talk with him. Maybe he has some details he forgot to mention."

Luca's door was shut. Vic knocked quietly. "You in there, champ?"

"No," said Luca.

Vic entered the room.

"Your mom and I have plenty of time to be mad later, but right now you need to tell me everything you know."

"Remember when we went to the Pirates game after Father's Day?"

"Sure. What about it?"

"Well, I left my window open a crack so the cats could get out. They kept pestering me about wanting to be outside. I let them back in, and there was no problem."

"Yeah, except wasn't that when everyone got fleas?"

"Oh, yeah, I had almost forgotten about that." Luca was digging himself a deeper hole.

"Okay, so, that was the first time. What about this time? Did they say where they were going?"

"No, but they promised they'd be back in a half-hour."

Vic sighed and rubbed his forehead. "Think, Luca. Did they say anything?"

Luca shook his head. He had never looked sadder.

"I don't care what my punishment is, Dad. I just want the cats to be okay."

Vic gave Luca a crooked grin, touched by his son's words, and then rejoined the other adults to map out a plan.

"I'm so sorry about what happened, guys," Vic said to Lisa and Keith. "If it's any consolation, he's beside himself with worry."

"We were 11 once, too, Vic," said Keith. "If I had a dime for every time I did something dumb when I was that age, I could retire tomorrow."

The four adults figured it would be best to take off in different directions, having no idea where their cats' curiosity would lead them.

"Should we print out their pictures and start stapling them to telephone poles?" asked Vic.

"Let's be optimistic. They couldn't have gotten that far, could they have? We'll do that if we have to," said Claudia.

They all bid each other good luck and headed off to find their wandering felines.

Meanwhile, Franklin was still fast asleep when Fatty picked up her head and said to the other two: "Listen. When he wakes up, we're normal cats. No talking."

The other two agreed, not sure what Fatty was up to but confident in her plan.

And Luca? He felt awful, but instead of wallowing in his misery, he got busy and put his construction skills to use.

THE FOUR CAT SEARCHERS were exchanging texts like crazy:

Anything?

No.

No.

Nothing.

You contact Luca?

Yep. Nothing on the home front.

I'm going to head back home and print out a picture of them.

Okay.

Sounds good.

The big stapler's in the kitchen.

Got it.

So, Vic raced back home, found a picture of all three of them from their first playdate, printed out 50 copies, grabbed the stapler, and started letting the area neighborhoods know of the cats' plight.

They kept searching, but their texts grew more pessimistic as the last of daylight evaporated.

Anything?

No.

No.

No.

They're not outside cats.

Not anymore, but Fatty was. She'll protect them.

You talk to Luca?

Yeah. Nothing.

The four kept searching, on foot and eventually by car, till almost midnight. Exhausted, they called it a night.

"We regroup when the sun rises," said Claudia.

They all agreed.

Luca was waiting for them when they got home. He was as doleful as when they had begun their search.

"Honey, we know how smart they are. They'll be back. And they probably have a great story to tell us," said Claudia.

"This is all my fault," he said.

"Don't worry about that now, champ," said Vic. "Just say a prayer for your friends' safety before you go to sleep, and tomorrow will be a better day."

Luca sauntered off to bed.

"You promise?" asked Claudia.

"What?"

"That tomorrow will be a better day."

"They're smart cats, Claud. We know how smart they are. Lisa and Keith don't, and we can't tell them. But I'm sure they're fine. They'll pop up."

Franklin awoke with a slight headache. But he also felt renewed—incredibly so.

He saw the cats around him, each with one eye closed and the other staring at him. "Ah, so, I didn't completely imagine you, but . . ."

He looked at Fatty. "So, portly friend, what have you to say for yourself?"

Fatty's countenance was as aloof as a cat's could be.

Franklin chuckled. "I dreamt you guys were talking to me." The chuckle grew into full laughter. "And you," he said, pointing at Fatty, "you knew everything about me! Even my wife's name."

He reached out a hand toward Fatty. She nudged him.

"I hurt you. I don't know who that monster was who did that to you, but—no, wait. That's not right. I accept full responsibility for my actions toward you. That monster was me. I was wrong. All I can do is ask for your forgiveness and hope you'll grant it."

Fatty hobbled up onto the old man's lap.

"I guess that means my request has been granted."

Franklin scritched Fatty's chin and said, "I have some important things to do today, dear, but my first order of business is finding out who you belong to. They must be worried sick."

Mrs. Garetti was getting her paper off the driveway when an orange cat tapping at the neighbor's window caught her eye.

When Red became aware of his audience, he used both front paws and began tapping frantically.

"Hello?"

"Martin? Hi. This is your father's neighbor."

"Yes, Mrs. Garetti?"

"Um, does your father have a cat?"

"Not that I'm aware of."

"Well, I was getting my paper this morning, and there was an orange-and-white cat sitting on his living-room windowsill. And he didn't seem particularly happy."

"Okay, thank you, Mrs. Garetti. I'll be over shortly."

"Dad has a cat, apparently."

"What?" asked Beth.

"I have no idea what's going on, but that was Mrs. Garetti. She said there's an unhappy cat sitting on Dad's living-room windowsill. Guess I'll go over and see what's going on."

"Be careful, honey. Maybe the cat's drunk, too."

Martin smiled. "Maybe I should bring a pair of gloves."

On his way to his father's house, Martin came across numerous "missing" signs. One of the cats pictured was orange and white. He figured this wasn't a coincidence.

Martin knocked on the front door, fearing the worst—a drunken father, catnip strewn across the floors—but was pleasantly surprised when a sober Franklin opened the door and greeted his son warmly.

"Dad, do you have a—"

"Cat? Yeah, three of them, apparently. I have a lot of explaining to do, son, but the first order of business is getting these cats back to their owner."

Martin handed his father one of the fliers.

"Yep, that's them, all right. Guess I should call the number."

Luca was finishing up his secret project when the phone rang. He almost tripped over his supplies, such was his rush to answer it.

"Hello?" he said.

"Yes. Hello, son. My name is Franklin Betters, and I believe I may have something that belongs to you. Is your mom or dad home?"

"Is it the cats?! Do you have the cats?" asked Luca.

"Yes, that's right. Are your pare—"

"No, they're out searching for them. I'll call them right now."

"Okay, listen. I live at 613 Manor. I'll be waiting for them."

"Are they okay?"

"Yes, son. They're fine."

"Thank you, thank you, thank you!"

Luca's fingers couldn't punch in the numbers fast enough.

"Hello?" said Vic.

"Dad! The cats! They're safe!"

"What? They came back?"

"No. They're with Franklin Betters. He lives at—"

"What? How does he have our cats?"

"I have no idea, but he says they're fine."

"That's great, honey. I'll tell the others, and we'll head over."

The group texts that followed:

Just talked to Luca. They're safe. They're with Franklin Betters over on Manor.

What? Who? They're okay?

Yep. Luca says they're fine.

Thank goodness!

Can't wait to see them!

And Vic and Claudia's private text exchange:

Looks like Fatty returned to the scene of sadness.

What was she thinking?!

Dunno. I'm sure they'll tell us!

And back to the group chat:

Listen, guys. I'm actually close to my house. I'll get the carriers, hop in the car, and meet you there. It's 613 Manor.

And that's what Vic did. And when he reached 613 Manor, he saw three incredibly happy adults approaching the front door.

Franklin opened the door and greeted them warmly.

"Hello, I'm Franklin Betters. Please come in. Now, I won't charge the three interlopers for their overnight stay, provided they give me good reviews on TripAdvisor."

They all laughed, and Martin ducked away because witnessing his father make a good-natured joke—the way he used to—was almost overwhelming. "It's Dad," he whispered to himself.

"I've been meaning to close that hole in the cellar window for months," said Franklin. "I guess they took advantage, and, well, curiosity got the best of them. I apologize for any stress this caused you."

"No, sir, no apologies necessary. There is an 11-year-old boy who has some explaining to do, though," said Claudia.

"Ah! He sounded very relieved when I told him I had the cats. Don't be too hard on him. We were all his age once."

"Yes, well, we'll get out of your hair. Um, it's none of my business, but that scratch under your eye doesn't have anything to do with the cats, does it?" asked Vic.

Franklin chuckled. "Well, I think I startled the fellow when I went down to the cellar to see what the noise was. No harm. He was just being a cat."

"Um, okay. Well, thanks again."

The three cats were loaded into two carriers, and off they went, with Claudia giving Red and Fatty a subtle high sign to remind them they still had to keep quiet.

"Talking cats, Martin."

"What's that, Dad?"

"Apparently, I was so drunk, I hallucinated that those cats were talking to me last night. And the chubby one? She knew everything about me, even your mother's name."

"So, all the pleading and yelling we've done over the years did nothing. It was talking cats to the rescue?"

"Son, at some level I knew you and your wife and sisters cared deeply. Everything you did came from a place of love. I was just too stubborn to pay heed. Can you find it in your heart to forgive an old man?"

"Of course, Dad."

The two embraced.

"And the chubby cat? That wasn't my first encounter with her. She snuck in a while ago, and I—I did something I'm not proud of. I hurt her."

"How?"

"I threw a candleholder at her. That's why she hobbles. But I asked for her forgiveness, and this may sound weird, but I think in some peculiar way she granted it to me."

"Well, think about it, Dad. Animals never start wars or steal your wallet. I think sometimes they're better than most of us."

Franklin nodded. "Listen. I can't wait to see your wonderful family and give them the biggest hug I can muster, but are you as hungry as I am? And do you still like French toast?"

"Yes. And yes."

THE GIOPPOLOS DROVE IN silence, partially because Vic and Claudia were upset at the cats, partially because the cats knew they had made a huge mistake, and partially because all of them were trying to process the whole thing.

It was Aurora who broke the silence.

"Listen," she said. "My humans are nothing but happy and relieved that I'm okay. When you drop me off, the three of us will resume our lives, and I'll get off scot-free because, as far as they know, I'm just a regular cat whose curiosity got the best of her."

She continued.

"Mr. and Mrs. Gioppolo, please don't be too mad at Luca. We badgered him into letting us out. We promised we'd be gone no more than a half-hour. And Fatty? Well, she was kind of awesome."

They reached the Robinsons' house, and off Aurora went, back to her normal-cat life until the next playdate.

The Gioppolos were alone and continued to travel in silence. The second they were home, though, and the cats were released from the carrier, the questioning commenced.

"What were any of you thinking?" asked Vic, as Luca gave the cats a huge embrace.

"We weren't, Dad. I never should have let them out."

"No, Luca," said Red, "it's my fault. Both trips were my idea."

"And I'm just as guilty for going along. The first time was fun, and I just figured the second trip would be more of the same," said Fatty.

Vic and Claudia were furious at all of them for this misadventure, but they also found themselves drowning in the glumness of three of the saddest faces one could imagine.

"How did you wind up there, anyway?" asked Vic.

"Well, I guess you could say curiosity," said Fatty. "Red wanted to see where I had holed up on cold nights, and I wanted to see if anything was different. We didn't plan on having an encounter."

"So," said Claudia, "what was Aurora talking about when she said you were awesome, Fatty?"

"You should have seen her, Mama!" said Red. "I think she changed that old dude's life. So, we sneak into his cellar, right? And we're walking around, and boom, there he is. And he calls Fatty fat. So, naturally, I jump on his face and—"

"Red!" yelled Claudia.

"Well, what was I supposed to do? He insulted my friend. Anyway, Fatty, as usual, can't keep quiet, and she yells, 'Red!'—kinda like you just did—and we're busted."

"He knows you talk?" asked Vic.

"Well, sorta, but he was drunk, right? And that's when Fatty hatches her plan. Because of the sad story you told us about him, we knew the details of his life. When Fatty mentioned Ruth, that was it. The old man figured he was so drunk, he was hallucinating."

"And then what happened, Fatty?" asked Vic.

"Well, I got him to talk about all his misdeeds. He seemed to grasp how off track his life had become. And Red got to him to apologize to me. And it was sincere."

"And then," Red continued, "he fell asleep. When he awoke, we were all normal cats, on Fatty's advice. I sat in the front window to get anyone's attention, and, well, here we are."

"All right, you three," said Claudia, "scram for a while. Your father and I have some discussing to do."

And the three did as they were told while the two-person judge and jury decided their fate.

Vic groaned. "You know what my mom would have done to me for such an escapade?"

"Strangled you?" asked Claudia.

"Nope. Private school. That was the go-to threat. My parents were going to send me to some far-off private school. Too bad I didn't have access to their tax records, or I would have known what an idle threat it was."

"So, you're proposing we send the cats to private school?"

"Yes, the esteemed Garfield Academy for Talking Felines. The meal plan consists entirely of lasagna. Honestly, I have no idea what to do. On one hand, they were all incredibly reckless, and the cats could have ended up hurt—or worse. And one of the cats isn't even ours. On the other, it appears Fatty saved an old man's life."

"No one ever said parenting's easy, babe," said Claudia. "And as far as we know, we're the only two parents of talking cats in the whole universe. There's no manual here."

"We'll think of something. Let's just enjoy the rest of the weekend," said Vic.

"He made me French toast," Martin said to Beth. "We laughed and had a wonderful conversation. It was like old times."

"And it's all because of a talking cat," said a wary Beth.

"Well, no, not quite. Yes, but the cat wasn't really talking. It was Dad hitting rock bottom and coming face-to-face with the brutal truth."

"Amazing. And you think it's for real?"

"Well, one day at a time, as the saying goes, but wait till you see him," said Martin. "I think you'll be pleasantly surprised."

And promptly at 2:00, just as he had promised, Franklin arrived at his son's house.

"Beth, dear," he said as he entered, "I braved the Black Friday crowds before I came here. This is for you."

Beth unwrapped the box, revealing her favorite chocolate truffles.

"You didn't have to do this," she said.

"You're right, dear," Franklin said. "This is a small gesture, enormously too small to make up for my behavior all these years. But it's a start and a promise. Can we begin fresh?"

"Oh, of course we can," said Beth, embracing her father-in-law.

"Now, where's that young lady?" asked Franklin.

"I'm right here, Grandpa," said Michaela as she entered the living room.

"And these are for you," said Franklin, handing his granddaughter a lovely fall arrangement of flowers.

"They're beautiful," she said.

"As beautiful as you are, Michaela." He looked directly at her. "My dear, by the simple fact that you're talking to me, I know what a good person you are and that you were raised right."

"What do you mean, Grandpa?"

"No, don't play nice with me. That old drunk doesn't deserve a scintilla of your respect. I almost killed you, Michaela." He paused to a whisper. "I almost killed you."

She looked away.

"No, look at me, sweetheart. I will never forgive myself for what I did to you. All I can do is humbly ask for your forgiveness and promise to do better."

Michaela nodded through her tears. "Of course I forgive you."

The two embraced tightly, and, for once, a visit from Franklin Betters wouldn't result in a silent car ride home but instead would end with a sober Franklin driving himself home, fighting back tears while saying, "In the time I have left, I'm going to make everything right, Ruth. You watch."

"WE'RE SORRY, LUCA," SAID Red. "It's like we can't help getting you in trouble."

"No, it's okay," said Luca. "I should have said no to you and Aurora. Who knows what could have happened to you guys? I'm just glad you're all safe."

"So, Luca, you have more experience in this department. What are they going to do to us?" asked Fatty.

"I don't honestly know. This is the worst thing I've ever done," he said. "In the past, if I backtalked to one of them or something like that, I'd get more chores or wouldn't be allowed to play video games for a couple days. But this is different."

The three of them grew silent, contemplating what Vic and Claudia would devise as punishment and fearing the worst.

"I bet we don't get snacks for a month," said Fatty.

"Or they won't let us play in boxes when they get packages," said Red. "They'll just cruelly rip up the sweet, new boxes in front of us, laughing manically as they do so."

"And I think I can kiss that Fender goodbye for Christmas," said Luca.

Meanwhile, 30 feet away, the Honorable Claudia and Vic worked out the details of a suitable sentence.

"No snacks for the cats for, what, three months?" said Vic.

"I don't know," said Claudia. "That seems mean. They love snacks. And let's not forget Fatty changed the course of someone's life."

"Yeah, you're right. Heck, I don't know. I know someone has his heart set on a new guitar for Christmas. Maybe that doesn't happen?"

"Vic, how would you feel on Christmas morning watching your son open up a box containing not a shining, new guitar but, I don't know, socks and a new hockey helmet?"

"Like the world's meanest parent? But, honey, he screwed up. Those cats could have been stolen or hurt. And what would we have said to Keith and Lisa if something had happened to Aurora? We were all worried sick. We didn't sleep the night they were missing. They can't walk free."

"Let me ask you a question, Vic. Does Luca feel horrible about what he did?"

"Absolutely."

"And how about the cats? How do they feel?"

"I think they realize what they did was wrong and dangerous."

"So, maybe we do nothing."

"No, Claudia. Nothing is not an option."

"Oh, let me finish, Hanging Judge Gioppolo. We do nothing. But we don't tell them this. We just keep them on edge for a while, wondering what their punishment will be."

"And their punishment will be contemplating the error of their ways until we reveal to them that that's the punishment itself?"

"Bingo."

"That's fiendish."

"Well, I prefer the word 'clever,' but I assume you're in?"

"Yes. How about 'fiendishly clever'?"

"Yeah, that works. So, mum's the word till, I don't know, Christmas Day?"

"We're going to have three very well-behaved children for the next month, aren't we?"

"Two furry angels and one decidedly less-furry angel."

ABOUT A WEEK LATER, Franklin contacted Vic and Claudia to see how the cats were. Vic told him they were fine, and Franklin asked if he could pay them all a visit. He had something for the cats.

On the day of the visit, Red and Fatty were told to be on their best behavior, since Vic and Claudia were concerned that Franklin might know the truth about them.

"Be extra normal, you two," said Vic.

"Papa, what does 'extra normal' mean?" asked Red.

"I have no clue, pal. Just be a cat. Do that stretching thing you do. Chase a ball of yarn but then stop suddenly for a quick bath. You know, normal but even more so."

"Just don't talk, you two," said Claudia. "Deal?"

"Mum's the word, Mom," said Fatty.

The doorbell rang, and Franklin stood on the front porch holding a small gift bag.

"Mr. Betters, please, come in," said Vic.

"Oh, please. Call me Franklin."

"Only if you call me Vic."

"It's a deal."

Franklin and Claudia exchanged pleasantries before Franklin got to the heart of his visit.

"Listen, folks. There's a reason I'm visiting you. My kids have dubbed it the Apology Tour." He chuckled. "It's possible you've heard some stories about me over the years."

Vic and Claudia nodded ever so slightly.

"No, it's okay, folks. But here it is from the horse's mouth, and I'll keep it as short as I can. My wife died the morning we were supposed to take a fabulous vacation. I was devastated and, over the years, became a

170

mean, old drunk. I alienated my family. I even hurt that sweet cat I see peering around the corner."

"That's Fatty," said Vic.

"Her name's Fatty?" asked Franklin.

"Yep. It was our son's idea, and, well, it kind of fits."

Franklin chuckled. "Well, I don't know how she wound up here, but I hurt her a while back when she was trying to escape the cold. I apologized to her, and I know it sounds crazy, but I think she accepted it. But my behavior was unacceptable, and I want to apologize to you fine folks, too."

"Oh, don't beat yourself up, Mr. Be—Franklin," said Claudia. "None of us is perfect."

"That Fatty is a special cat," said Franklin. "When Fatty and her pals—"

"Red and Aurora," said Vic as Red entered the kitchen.

"Ah, that must be Red," said Franklin. "Anyway, on Thanksgiving, I had put on another scene with my family, and when I got home that night, I continued drinking and didn't stop till I heard a noise in the basement."

He looked away.

"This is kind of embarrassing to admit, folks, but I was so drunk I hallucinated that the three of them started talking to me. And they knew things about me! It was like Fatty was my therapist."

Vic and Claudia chuckled at this, in the hopes of pleasantly playing along with Franklin's story, but Vic laughed perhaps a beat too long and too loudly.

"It's not that funny, son," said Franklin.

"Well, no, of course. It's just—the thing about, you know, the cats and the talking and—"

"And this is our son, Luca," said Claudia as Luca came down the steps at precisely the right second.

"Ah, never have I heard a person sound more relieved than when I told you your cats were safe," said Franklin. "I hope your punishment wasn't too severe for letting them out."

"Actually, sir, I have no idea what my punishment is," said Luca.

Franklin slyly winked at Claudia, innately knowing what Vic and Claudia were up to.

"So, I come bearing gifts for the felines," said Franklin. "I'll never forgive myself for what I did to Fatty, but I hope that she and I—and all of us—can be friends from now on."

And from the bag, he pulled three fat catnip mice. The cats quickly approached.

"This is for you, Red. This is for you, dear Fatty. And this one is for your pal."

The cats indeed were in "extra normal" mode, as they chased their new toys throughout the downstairs.

"That was very sweet of you, Franklin," said Vic.

Franklin laughed as the cats continued their chasing. "You know, maybe getting a cat wouldn't be a bad idea. I could use the companionship when my family isn't around to pester."

"That's a great idea, Franklin," said Claudia. "Just make sure you get one that talks."

They all laughed, with Vic keeping his mirth in check this time upon feeling Claudia's eyes burn holes into him.

"Well, folks, thanks for your hospitality," said Franklin, "but my apology tour continues. I've spent the past week returning Frisbees and various balls to neighborhood kids. For the most part, the 'kids' are now adults and no longer reside there, but their parents appreciate the gesture. It gives them a chuckle."

"Please stay in touch, Franklin."

"Oh, I plan on doing just that, Vic," said Franklin. "I have a lot of living to do."

"And this time, young man," said Lisa, "don't let these three out. This is an indoor playdate."

Luca forced himself to smile, knowing she meant well. "I've learned my lesson, Mrs. Robinson."

"I'm sure you have," she said.

"All right, buddy," said Claudia. "We'll be out for a while. Remember to give Aurora her new catnip mouse, and your father is working but grab him if something comes up."

"Got it, Mom."

As soon as Lisa and Claudia departed, Aurora inquired about the catnip mouse.

"It's from Franklin, Mom," said Red. "He brought them over the other day for us. He still feels bad about what he did to Fatty."

And off Aurora went, chasing her new toy. Red and Fatty followed suit, each holding the mice in their mouths. They zoomed up and down the steps and through the first floor repeatedly, until they were all finally tired.

"Hey, Luca," said Red, "any chance you could let us out for a while?"

"That's not even remotely funny, dude," said Luca. "But we do have a fenced-in backyard. If you really need to feel the grass under your paws once in a while, I'm sure Mom and Dad would let you out, as long as you promised not to wander."

Red and Fatty looked at each other as if to say, "How come we never thought of that?"

"You're a smart boy, Luca," said Red. "And that's a great idea. I hope Mama and Papa don't fill your stocking with coal because of our latest escapade."

"Yeah, guys, I honestly don't know what they're up to," said Luca. "I just wish they would hand down their verdict, and we could deal with it. It's the not knowing that's the worst."

"It must be nice for you, Mom," said Red. "Your humans were so happy to have you back, they probably showered you with extra treats and hugs."

"They did, actually," she said. "But this whole thing has got me to thinking. I think they have a right to know about us."

"They do, Mom, but you have to be careful. Don't forget what happened when Fatty blabbed our secret while Papa was behind the wheel."

"Again with this, Red?" asked Fatty.

"I'm just sayin', pal," said Red.

"I'll admit that Red has a point, Aurora," said Fatty. "Finding out your cat talks in a moving vehicle is probably not ideal. And Claudia almost passed out when she heard us. And she was at home."

"Maybe Mom and Dad should be the ones to tell them," said Luca. "It might make for an easier transition than you just blurting out human words, Aurora."

"Our bro is so smart," said Red. "That's another splendid idea. I hope Santa's keeping a scorecard."

"Let's talk to Dad and see what he thinks," said Luca.

"Uh-oh, the whole gang's here," said Vic. "No, you most definitely cannot go outside."

"I want to tell Keith and Lisa the truth," said Aurora. "I don't like keeping secrets from them."

"And Luca here suggested that it might make it easier—and safer—if the news came from you and Mama," said Red. "That's a smart boy you're raising."

"Yeah, that is a good idea, Luca. Well, we'll have you all over for dinner, and we can gently give them the shock of their lives."

"Thank you, Mr. Gioppolo."

And thus it was arranged. The Robinsons came over for dinner, with Aurora in tow, like they had done numerous times over the last several months. They had Chinese takeout and a couple of beers. They joked around while the cats played. They halfheartedly watched the Pens game. It was a completely routine dinner among friends. Until it wasn't.

VIC AND CLAUDIA SPENT hours trying to find the perfect words to mini-mize the shock their friends were about to endure.

"How about 'There's something you don't know about your cat'?" suggested Vic.

"I don't know," said Claudia. "That kind of builds up the tension. We're trying to reduce it."

"Okay, well, how about, 'Hey, guys, you don't know this, but your cat talks. And so do our cats. Welcome to CrazyTown, Population: Us.'"

"That's a bit too direct."

They went back and forth with ideas, but whatever either of them suggested didn't capture the situation to their liking.

"Well," said Claudia, "at least they'll be sitting on a couch. If either of them faints, they'll be close to the floor already."

"We'll know when the time is right, and we'll be as gentle as we can be," said Vic.

So, the second period came to an end, and there was a lull in the conversation. The cats were nearby.

"Guys," said Vic, "there's something we need to tell you. And it's not easy to say."

Keith and Lisa were suddenly concerned.

"No," said Claudia, sensing their tension, "it's not a bad thing. In fact, it's awesome. It's just . . . surprising."

"Startling, even," said Vic.

"Yes! Yes, startling—that's the word," said Claudia.

"We're all ears," said Lisa.

Vic and Claudia exchanged glances, knowing the next words they spoke would forever alter their friends' lives.

"Aurora talks. So do Red and Fatty," said Claudia.

"You mean like meow-meow-meow stuff?" asked Keith.

"Nope. I mean English," said Claudia.

Keith and Lisa chuckled nervously, not knowing what to make of their friends' announcement.

"April 1st isn't for a few months, guys," said Keith.

Vic and Claudia motioned to Aurora, who promptly jumped onto Lisa's lap.

"Hi, Mom," she said.

And before he could fully grasp what was occurring, Keith found himself trying to catch a suddenly airborne Aurora while simultaneously preventing his wife from sliding to the floor.

"Wha—what is going on?" he said to no one in particular.

Lisa regained her stability, and she, her husband, and their talking cat sat in silence for a moment.

"Don't be afraid, Mr. and Mrs. Robinson," said Fatty.

"Ah, I knew Fatty had to blurt something out," said Red. "Just like with Franklin. And, guys, you should have seen what happened when Papa found out about us. We were all in the car, and he almost ran over a family of pandas crossing the road."

"Really, Red? Pandas? In Pennsylvania?" asked Fatty.

"They could have been zoo escapees, pal," said Red. "Anyway, the point is, Mr. and Mrs. Robinson, we talk, and Chatty Fatty likes to spill the beans."

The Robinsons continued sitting in silence, running through the options of what could possibly be occurring.

"Are we having a—" Lisa began to say.

"A dream? Nope. That was my first thought, too," said Vic. "Also, you didn't have one too many beers, and neither of you is spontaneously insane."

"Do they sing, too?" asked Keith, who was not really sure what to say but felt that talking would help him keep a grip on reality, flimsy as it may be.

"I've been known to accompany Luca on guitar," said Fatty.

Lisa and Keith were now staring at Claudia and Vic, desperate for an explanation.

"We don't know," said Vic. "The cats don't know. It just . . . is."

"When Mom and I were at the shelter," said Red, "we were the only ones who talked. When you took her, I was heartbroken."

"We're sorry, Red," said Lisa. "Wait. Am I in conversation with a cat?"

"You are, ma'am," said Red. "But no worries. Mama and Papa tracked Aurora down, and now everyone's happy."

"I still feel like I'm in a really weird dream, guys," said Keith.

"Yeah, the effects will linger for a while," said Vic. "But eventually it will all seem very normal. Trust us."

"You could have told us before, you know," said Lisa.

"Yeah, but we felt that it was Aurora's call to make," said Claudia. "Plus, we needed to make sure we trusted you."

"Trusted us? What does that mean?" asked Lisa.

"Think about it, honey," said Keith. "We could be filthy rich."

"Bingo," said Claudia. "Vic had some fantasy about tooling around town in a—what was it?—Minion-yellow Jaguar?"

"They make yellow Jaguars?" asked Keith.

"When you're crazy-rich, you can get a yellow Jaguar," said Vic.

"But our lives would be entirely disrupted—not to mention the cats' lives—and for what?" asked Claudia. "We decided we liked our quiet lives just the way they were."

"I think we're all on the same page," said Lisa.

"So, no one knows about this besides us?" asked Keith.

"Nope," said Claudia.

"But what was Red saying about Fatty blurting something out when they were stuck at the old man's house?" asked Lisa.

"Ah, yes, Franklin," said Vic. "They did talk in front of him, but he was quite drunk at the time, and he convinced himself it was a hallucination. He's changed his ways as a result of the incident."

"The talking cats are a force of good," said Lisa.

"And endless entertainment," said Claudia.

"I still can't wrap my head around this," said Keith. "Maybe they all talk, and these two slipped up in front of you?"

"Well, that's partially true," said Vic. "Luca was the first to catch them talking. They thought he was at school, he wasn't, and that's a very long story we'll share with you another day."

"Mom and I were the only two at the shelter who talked," said Red. "Believe me. We tried engaging the others, but they were just meow-meow cats."

"And I lived outside a long time and never came across another talking cat or dog or bug or bird or anything," said Fatty.

"If any of the birds had yelled, 'Please don't eat me!', would you have listened, Fatty?" asked Red.

She bared her teeth in his direction. He jumped back.

"So, somehow, in our small city of not even 15,000 people reside the world's only known talking felines," said Keith.

"Apparently," said Vic.

"And this makes sense to you?" asked Keith.

"Not in the least," said Vic. "But life is full of mysteries."

"The shelter doesn't know that they talk?" asked Keith.

"Not a clue," said Red.

"Aurora, honey, how did you wind up at the shelter?" asked Keith.

"I don't know. We were outside briefly, and then someone came along and scooped us up," said Aurora. "And then we were at the shelter. And then you showed up."

"And you, Fatty?" asked Keith. "Do you remember being anywhere but outside?"

"I don't," said Fatty. "I lived my entire life outside. And then one day, I came upon this house, and Red and I instantly knew."

"Astonishing," said Keith.

"Like I said, you'll get used to it," said Vic.

"I suppose the playdates are going to get a lot louder now," said Lisa.

"You are correct, ma'am," said Red. "I never shut up."

"I think we need to head home," said Keith. "There's a lot to process here."

"Thank you, Mr. and Mrs. Gioppolo, for helping out tonight," said Aurora.

"Oh, it was our pleasure. And it was Luca's idea," said Vic. "He thought it might be safer if you heard it from us instead of directly from Aurora. The three of us weren't so lucky."

"Well, thank you for a lovely and unforgettable evening," said Lisa.

"Good night, Red," said Aurora.

"Good night, Mom," said Red. "And remember, Mrs. Robinson, the next playdate's at your house. It'll be loud!"

And Lisa and Keith headed into the night, their heads full of questions they would not get answers to. They were equal parts delighted and perplexed, unsure of what was happening but glad that another family was going through the exact same circumstances.

WHILE VIC AND CLAUDIA were enjoying date night, Luca decided to make a special Christmas present for his parents. He asked his father if he could borrow his phone while they were out, and now all he needed was the cats to behave.

"All right, you two. I've written a song, and I thought you might be able to supply me with some Christmas-themed lyrics."

He played the song for them. It was an upbeat tune that he had been working on for months.

"That's lovely, Luca," said Fatty.

"So, how about some lyrics? And then we can record it," said Luca.

"Okay, I'm thinking something with 'Fatty Claus,'" said Red.

"Well, that's funny, because I was thinking 'Reddy the orange-nosed doofus' might fit in nicely," said Fatty.

"Enough, you two," said Luca. "They're not going to be out that long, and this is a present for them. We've put them through a lot this year."

Chastened, the cats put their heads together and, along with Luca's assistance, came up with the following:

> First came Reddy
> He was from the shelter
> Then came Fatty
> Who would hide in a cellar
>
> But now they're both here
> They want to bring you some cheer
> 'Cause it's Christmas, Christmas
> And you both are so dear
>
> Reddy likes to jump
> Fatty's more earthbound
> And Luca plays guitar
> What a beautiful sound

Now everyone's here
No need for a tear
'Cause it's Christmas, Christmas
Will you lend us an ear?

Red and Fatty
Wait for their Christmas prosciutto
What rhymes with prosciutto?
I dunno. Pseudo and Pluto?

Well, that's pretty near
There's no need for fear
'Cause it's Christmas, Christmas
And our love is sincere

"Guys, I think this is pretty great," said Luca. "But you know what would make it even better?"

The cats shook their heads.

"Wait here. I'll be right back."

And down to the basement he scampered. Rummaging through the boxes of Christmas decorations, he found exactly what he was looking for: Santa hats on stuffed animals, which he quickly borrowed.

"Would either of you be interested in wearing—"

And before he could finish his sentence, the cats grabbed the caps from Luca and promptly placed them on their heads.

Luca set up the phone, and after only three takes—on the first take, Red tried ad-libbing a verse centered around his awesomeness, and on the second Fatty was so into singing her hat fell off—the task was complete. Within minutes, they heard the car pulling into the driveway.

"Okay, Dad, here's your phone. Thanks. We made a video. Promise me you won't look at it till Christmas."

"You have my word, buddy," said Vic.

"Can't wait to see what you three came up with," said Claudia.

"It's awesome, Mama," said Red. "Especially my part."

"Well, that goes without saying, doesn't it, Red?" asked Vic.

"You know me so well, Papa."

Luca and the cats dashed off, happy in their accomplished mission and hopeful that Vic and Claudia would keep their promise.

"This is going to kill me, Claud," said Vic.

"Yeah, but it's only two weeks," said Claudia.

"Can we maybe take a little peek?" asked Vic.

"What are you, seven?" asked Claudia.

"Do you know any 7-year-olds whose hair is starting to turn gray?" asked Vic.

"No. And, honey? It's more than starting," said Claudia. "It's darn near completing."

"Thanks, babe. You know Santa watches adults, too, right? I'd hate to see you wind up on the 'naughty' list.

"Vic, we've never used our fireplace, and we've never had it cleaned. So, if the portly man in the red suit wants to take a chance struggling down our chimney, he's in for one nasty surprise. Besides, the gray makes you look distinguished."

"Ooh, someone just got the call up to the 'nice' list. Pack your bags, little lady. No more dingy buses and 12-hour rides for you. First-class chartered flights going forward."

"I do wonder what they came up with, though," said Claudia.

"Uh, didn't we just have this conversation? Remember? You asked if I was seven."

"You know, now that you mention it, I do recall that conversation," Claudia said. "Just put the phone away. Hide it for a while. Out of sight, out of mind."

And Vic stashed his phone in an office desk drawer and joined the rest of the family to watch "The Grinch."

THE NEXT EVENING, THERE was a knock at the door.

"We're not expecting anyone," said Vic, "so best behavior, you two."

"Got it, Papa," said Red.

Vic opened the door and saw a man slightly older than himself staring back.

"You must be Vic," said the man.

"That's right. What can I do for you?"

"My name's Martin Betters. I think you and your cats have had some interaction with my father recently."

"Oh, yes, indeed we have. Please come in."

"Thanks."

"Ah, those are the famous talking cats, eh?" said Martin, spotting Red and Fatty lounging on the living-room rug.

Vic made sure to temper his nervous laughter down to a pleasing chuckle.

"Yep, that's them all right."

"I hope I didn't catch you at a bad time," said Martin, "but I wanted to personally thank you—and the cats—for what you've done for my father. The change in him is nothing short of remarkable."

"Well, Martin, I had nothing to do with it. But Claudia and I are glad to have met your dad. He's a great guy."

"And he's become quite smitten with your cats," said Martin. "So, were they shelter cats or . . .?"

"Well, Fatty was a stray who showed up in our backyard, but Red was from the nearby shelter. They always have cats in need of homes."

"Awesome. I think Dad and I will swing by someday soon. Well, thanks for your time, and it was nice meeting you, Red and Fatty."

Vic held his breath for fear that one of them would respond, but they played it cool and behaved as though they were regular, aloof cats enjoying a nap.

"Pleasure, Martin," said Vic. "Whenever you're in town to visit your dad, don't be a stranger."

"You bet, Vic. Have a great day."

"Franklin is a good man, isn't he, Kind Sir?" asked Fatty.

"He is."

"But he did some bad things, didn't he?"

"He did, Fatty," said Vic. "Humans are complex and imperfect. He took a huge body blow when his wife passed, and for a while he wasn't himself. But he didn't get knocked out. And now he's back on his feet, in no small part because of some cat I know."

"I helped, too, Papa," said Red.

"You jumped on his face, Red," said Fatty.

"That probably woke him up. And then you swooped in and talked some sense into him. It was a team effort," said Red. "Anyway, I'm glad he's going to visit the shelter. I hope he gets a couple of us."

The smell of cookies being baked lured Fatty into the kitchen.

"Hey, Mom," she said. "Did you know we had a visitor just now?"

"Yeah, I heard," said Claudia, "but my fingers were full of cookie dough. Franklin's son, eh?"

"Yep. And did you hear? They're going to take a trip to the shelter and rescue a cat."

"That's nice, sweetie. I bet it doesn't talk, though."

Fatty chuckled. "Yeah, probably not. So, what are you making?"

"Well, I have the last batch of chocolate-chip cookies in the oven, and now I'm going to start on sugar cookies."

"It's a good thing cats don't have sweet tooths, Mom, or I'd be even bigger."

"Well," said Vic, entering the kitchen and quickly swiping a handful of cookies, "I do have a sweet tooth, and when I was a kid I got made fun of for being, well, let's say husky."

"Husky?" asked Fatty.

"Yeah, when I was a kid, blue jeans came in three sizes—slim, regular, and husky. I always got the husky—until I was 11. That summer, I lost some weight, and for the first time in my life, I could wear 'regular' jeans. I was so happy."

"But weren't you still the same person?" asked Fatty.

"Sure. There was just less of me."

"But if everyone were regular, the world would be a less-interesting place, wouldn't it?" asked Fatty.

"Yeah, Fatty," said Claudia "that's an excellent point. How'd you get so wise?"

"I don't think I'm wise, Mom, but living outside all those cold nights makes me appreciate what I have now. It's like Franklin. He almost lost everything that mattered to him, and now he realizes how fortunate he is."

"Yep, Fatty," said Vic. "Appreciate what you have, never take anything for granted, and if I keep eating these cookies, I'm going to be wearing husky pants again."

Fatty laughed. "I'm going to go see what Red's up to," she said.

"Okay, sweetheart," said Claudia.

"Fatty has a way of putting a smile on my heart."

"I know what you mean, Claud. And we're one day closer to seeing what's on my phone."

"You've resisted the temptation?"

"Absolutely, babe."

"You better be telling the truth," said Luca as he entered the kitchen.

"Ah, there's my assistant," said Claudia. "And just in time. What are we doing—Santas, trees, deer, stars?"

"All of them, Mom."

Vic grabbed a few more chocolate-chip cookies as he departed, but his eyes lingered for a moment as he watched his wife and son, knowing that Luca wouldn't be 11 forever.

"Vic? It's Franklin Betters. How are you doing?"

"Very well, sir," said Vic. "What's up?"

"Hey, listen. Some evening this week, I would like you and your family to pay me a visit."

"Sure. Does Thursday work for you?"

"Yes, absolutely. Oh, and bring the four-legged members of your clan, too."

"Will do, Franklin. See you then."

"You bet."

"Hey, gang, that was Franklin Betters," said Vic. "He's invited us over, and he means all of us."

"Cool," said Red. "We can show you the exact place I jumped on his face and then heroically flagged for help."

"And Fatty can show us the place where she changed Franklin's life," said Claudia.

"Yeah, well, like I said, it was a team effort," said Red.

"Red, don't you see what this means?" asked Fatty, ignoring her pal's Red-centric version of the story.

Red gasped. "He has new cat friends!"

"I believe you're right," said Vic. "And it goes without saying that you guys are in normal mode every second we're there."

"Of course, Papa," said Red.

"Fatty, dear, are you okay with going back over there?" asked Claudia.

"Sure, Mom," said Fatty. "He's changed his ways. He's not the mean two-legged anymore."

"Ah, the infamous two-legged," said Vic.

"Fatty," said Claudia, "did you ever in your wildest dreams when you were living outside think you'd be paying the 'mean two-legged' a friendly visit?"

"Nope. I guess you just never know how things are going to turn out."

Thursday evening finally arrived. The cats were excited to pay Franklin—and his new friend or friends—a visit, even if it meant being carted around in their carriers for the brief trip.

"Okay, you two," said Vic as they pulled out of the driveway, "get all your words out now, because as soon as we enter Franklin's house, all I want to hear out of you is the occasional meow."

"Shoo-ba-dee-bah-bah-dee-boop-ba-loo-how-do-you-do,"   sang Red. "Okay, Papa, that oughta hold me for a few hours."

Vic sighed. "It had better, pal."

This was the same address they visited only a few weeks earlier, yet it was like stepping into an entirely new place. Everything was tidier. The family pictures on the walls were straighter. And scampering around the first floor were three cats. This was no longer a house. This was Franklin's home.

"Franklin, we brought you some cookies," said Claudia.

"Oh, thank you, dear. I'm glad you all could make it, especially you two," Franklin said, pointing at Red and Fatty.

"Martin and I took a trip to the shelter last week. My intention was to get one cat. This fella here caught my attention immediately because he seemed like he needed a home. The volunteers told me his sad story—many had tried to give him a forever home, and all had failed—but, if anything, that made me want to take him even more."

"It's Sunset!" Red wanted to scream.

"If anyone understands the power of second chances—or third or fourth ones, for that matter—it's me. Everyone, I'd like you to meet Sunrise."

"Oh, that's good!" Red wanted to yell.

And Sunrise promptly approached Red and gave him a nudge, as if to say, "Hey, I remember you," and then returned to Franklin.

"He's been an absolute sweetheart," said Franklin.

"Maybe he just needed the right home," said Claudia.

"So, I was good with Sunrise," said Franklin, "but then these two caught my eye. The volunteers told me they were new arrivals and that they were abandoned in a box on the side of a road. They were under-weight when the staff took them in, and since they were a mother and kitten, the staff was trying to keep them together."

"I love you, two-legged," Red wanted to shout.

"Please meet Faith and Hope, everyone," said Franklin.

And for the next several minutes, Red, Fatty, Sunrise, Faith, and Hope ran around Franklin's home, chasing catnip mice, chasing each other, and being nothing but normal, happy housecats.

"Well, it looks like Red and Fatty have some new friends," said Vic.

"They're welcome anytime, as are you fine folks," said Franklin. "Listen. Would it be okay if I stop by sometime Christmas morning? I have a little something for the cats."

"Of course! We'll be there," said Claudia.

"Well, you two, it looks like you're played out," said Vic. "Let's leave Franklin and his new friends in peace."

Red and Fatty dutifully made their way into their carriers, with Red barely able to keep quiet much longer.

Finally, when they were all safely inside the car, Red yelled out, "Guys, that's Sunset!"

"Who's Sunset, Reddy?" asked Claudia.

"He's a dude who left and came back I don't know how many times," said Red. "It never worked out for his humans. And every time he came back, he was a little more surly than I remembered him being. We all gave him wide berth at the shelter."

"And just to be clear—and I can't believe I have to ask this—he doesn't talk, right?"

"Nope. Not with words, anyway. He used to growl a lot at the shelter, though."

"Not too long ago, that same person was throwing things at me because I was simply trying to stay warm in his basement," said Fatty. "And now he has a houseful of cats, and he loves them."

"And he has Christmas presents for us, too," said Red.

"Oh, that's right. You heard what he was saying," said Vic. "You two were so good at being normal cats, I almost forgot you're anything but."

"Are you saying we're not normal, Kind Sir?" asked Fatty.

"You two are gloriously un-normal," said Claudia.

"And don't forget handsome, Mama," said Red.

"How could I ever forget that?" said Claudia.

"Fatty! Fatty!"

"What, Red?"

"Merry Christmas, pal!"

"Oh, same to you. What time is it?"

"I have no idea," said Red. "But it's still dark out. Maybe we should go ask Luca."

"Or maybe we should go back to sleep," said Fatty. "Everything is quiet. Let's just wait a bit more."

"Yeah, you're probably right," said Red.

So, both cats lay very still for what felt like an eternity but, in reality, was no more than ten minutes.

"You think we can go ask Luca now?" asked Red.

"I don't see why not," said Fatty. "We've been patient."

So, the two made their way into Luca's room, hopped on his bed, and began kneading his chest.

"Guys, it's, like, 6:18," said Luca. "Go back to your beds."

"Come on, bro," said Red. "Tell us you weren't already awake."

Luca laughed. "Yeah, since 5:30. But Mom and Dad are still quiet. Let's just hang together."

And they did just that. Luca, flanked by Red and Fatty, did their best to resume sleeping. All failed spectacularly.

"I can't wait for Mama and Papa to see our song," said Red.

"I hope they like it," said Fatty.

"Oh, they'll love it," said Luca.

Meanwhile, twenty feet away, Vic and Claudia were whispering, in an effort to avoid detection.

"The cats are in Luca's room," said Claudia.

"Yep. Little cat feet aren't completely silent," said Vic.

"Let's enjoy a few more moments of peace, babe," said Claudia.

"Agreed. The second one of our feet hits the floor, the gig's up," said Vic.

So, the five members of the Gioppolo family all lay in silence, with the three youngest members waiting to hear the green light of a foot creaking on hardwood.

They didn't have to wait long.

"I really could use some tea," said Claudia.

"Yeah, and those cookies are calling me," said Vic.

Gently placing one foot on the floor, Vic whispered, "How far do you think we'll get—" before Red, Fatty, and Luca came barreling into the bedroom.

"Not very far," said Claudia. "Your feet must have become husky overnight."

"Be nice," said Vic. "It's Christmas."

"Mama, Papa, Merry Christmas!" said Red.

"Yes, Merry Christmas to all of you," said Vic.

There were hugs all around.

"Your father and I were just heading to the kitchen for tea and cookies," said Claudia. "Do you think we should check to see if Santa swung by?"

Luca and the cats were halfway down the steps before Claudia finished her sentence.

"We could close the door and go back to sleep," said Vic.

"Merry Christmas, babe," said Claudia.

They kissed.

"Let's join the fray," said Vic.

"All right, you guys, let's let Luca go first," said Claudia, "since he's been here longer than you two."

Luca worked his way through the small gifts—a monthly guitar wall calendar, a tin of his favorite cashews, some clothes—saving the big box for last.

He paused before unwrapping the large, rectangular box and smiled.

"What are you waiting for, pal?" asked Vic.

"Well, I just thought maybe because of what happened at Thanksgiving—"

"Open the box, sweetie," said Claudia.

And he did. And there it was: a gleaming red Stratocaster.

"Thank you, thank you, thank you!" said Luca.

"You're welcome," said Vic. "Fill our home with beautiful music."

"I will, Dad!"

"Oh, and you might need this, too," said Claudia, sliding another sizable box his way.

"Sweet! An amplifier," said Luca.

"Bro, you're going to be rocking," said Red.

"I guess I'll have to sing louder now," said Fatty.

Claudia slid two small boxes the cats' way.

"Here, you two," she said. "This is your first gift."

The cats clawed through the wrapping paper, and Luca helped them with the box lids. Inside were two little Santa caps, with their names stitched into the white part.

Luca secured the hats onto the cats' heads.

"We're wearing these all day," said Red.

"All season," said Fatty.

"Be honest, guys," said Red. "Am I even more handsome wearing a cap?"

"I didn't think it possible," said Claudia, "but yes, I'd say you're downright dashing."

"Thank you, Mama. Anyone else want to chime in with a compliment?"

"Not particularly, Red," said Vic, "but we do have something else for you in the kitchen."

The cats followed Vic into the kitchen, where he procured two lunchmeat bags secured with festive red ribbons from the fridge.

"Sweet! Christmas prosciutto breakfast," said Red.

"You each get a pound, and yes, you can both have some now," said Vic. "Don't gorge yourselves. This should last you guys a while."

"And when you're done," said Luca, "there might be one more present for you guys."

The cats exchanged glances, stuffing their faces while anticipating what Luca had for them.

They hurried back to the living room, where Luca prepared to help them unveil their last gift.

"But before you tear off the paper," said Claudia, "there's a story behind this gift."

"Remember your Thanksgiving adventure?" asked Vic.

"Hard to forget," said Red.

"Well, Luca was a nervous wreck, as we all were," said Claudia, "but he decided to put his nerves to use in the most constructive way imaginable."

And with that, the cats, with Luca's help, unveiled a double-decker cardboard bus, with their names and caricatures emblazoned on the side. It was sturdily built, with thick cardboard tubes connecting the levels. And the top tier was reinforced and would be able to support both cats when they decided to travel topside. They both quickly hopped in.

"Bro, this is awesome," said Red.

"Luca, we can go on so many cool adventures now," said Fatty.

Vic began twirling his phone while clearing his throat.

"Oh, yeah! That's right," said Luca. "You can play the video now."

The cats quickly exited their bus, wanting to get close to Claudia and Vic as they played their song.

"Hi, Mom and Dad," said Luca on the video. "We know we gave you a heck of a scare recently, and we know we sometimes don't make the best decisions. But we love you, and we hope you like our song."

First came Reddy

He was from the shelter

Then came Fatty

Who would hide in a cellar . . .

And the song continued. And Vic and Claudia did their level best to not cry and largely succeeded. Once in a great while, something touches your heart so deeply that words can't suffice, and tears rush in to fill the void. Explaining this to an 11-year-old—not to mention two talking cats—was just too much of a task on Christmas morning.

"It's beautiful, you three," Vic said, clearing his throat.

"Best Christmas present ever," said Claudia.

The parents took a moment to regain their composure. They had an announcement to make.

"Before you do your Hendrix impression," said Vic, "and before you two head off to imaginary lands in your new vehicle, we do have one more gift for all three of you."

And Claudia entered the living room carrying a large, square box.

Luca and the cats quickly tore off the paper, popped the lid, and found themselves staring into an empty box.

The cats quickly jumped in, but the three of them were quite confused.

Vic and Claudia said nothing for a minute.

"I don't get it," said Luca.

"It's your punishment for Thanksgiving," said Claudia.

"Okay . . . I still don't get it."

"Well, for a month, you guys have been worried about what your punishment would be, right?" asked Vic.

"Yes," said Luca.

"Well, that was your punishment."

"The worrying about our punishment was our punishment?" asked Fatty.

"Yes," said Claudia. She was smiling.

"That's fiendish, Mama," said Red.

"Yeah, that's what I said," said Vic. "And remember, Luca, if this scene comes up in therapy someday, it was all your mother's idea."

Claudia playfully slapped her husband on the arm.

"So, we don't have to worry anymore?" asked Luca.

"You are free to resume your life," said Vic. "But go get ready for church."

There was a knock at the door.

"Ah, that must be Franklin," said Claudia.

"Merry Christmas, Claudia," said Franklin.

"Same to you. Please come in."

"I don't want to take too much of your time," he said, "but I wanted to give our four-legged friends a little treat. Was Santa good to them?"

"Yep," said Vic. "They got the prosciutto they asked fo—that we knew they liked."

"Prosciutto?" asked Franklin. "That's adorable."

"Yeah, they tasted it a few months ago and couldn't get enough of it," said Claudia.

"Well, this is for them," said Franklin, handing Claudia a bag of holiday-shaped cat treats. "I see they're enjoying cardboard."

"Yes, Luca made it for them. Is your family coming over to your house?" asked Claudia.

"Yes, all of them," said Franklin. "I have to get back and get the turkey in the oven. Have a wonderful Christmas."

"You, too" said Vic and Claudia together.

As soon as the door closed, Red said, "You almost blew our cover, Papa."

"Yeah, I'm aware, Reddy," said Vic, "but thanks for pointing it out."

"How long does Christmas church last?" asked Red.

"At least an hour," said Claudia. "Why do you ask?"

"I want to know how many adventures Fatty and I can go on," said Red. "Come on, pal. Let's explore the top level of our bus."

So, while the three humans went to Christmas service, Fatty and Red enjoyed fabulous explorations in their new double-decker and the empty punishment box, while sneaking in the occasional nibble of prosciutto.

FRANKLIN'S FAMILY WOULD BE arriving any minute. The turkey was resting on the counter. His kids promised to supply all the side dishes and desserts. He took a minute to look around his house. He couldn't believe what he was seeing.

For the first time since Ruth had passed, there was a Christmas tree standing in the living room. It was decorated with the standard sparkly bulbs, but a substantial part of it was adorned with his kids' youthful artwork. When he unearthed the holiday decorations from the basement, it had been so long, it was as if he was seeing them for the first time.

Along the mantel were stockings for each of his children and grandchildren. He even had stockings made for his new pals, Sunrise, Hope, and Faith.

The dining-room table was set from memory, the way Ruth would do it. It may not have been perfect, but it was close enough, and he certainly had given it his best. He knew she would have approved.

He even decorated outside. The warmer-than-normal weather enabled Franklin to cover every available tree, shrub, and bush with lights. On more than one occasion, he caught a neighbor sneaking a peek, no doubt baffled that "Old Man Bitters" was celebrating Christmas. He tried not to laugh.

And one by one, they arrived. There were hugs all around. Most of them hadn't met the cats, so introductions were in order. And they ate and laughed and reminisced about old times. At one point during the proceedings, Franklin interrupted his family to make an announcement.

"If you could excuse me for a moment, I'd like to say a few words. This has been the happiest holiday I've had since my dear Ruth passed away. Seeing you all here puts a song in my heart. But let's not ignore the elephant in the room. And that would be me, or, more to the point, the old me. You all remember him, right? The one who ruined countless holidays. The one who didn't realize how blessed he was. Don't be afraid to mention him, okay? I can take it. I'm not proud of the way I behaved, and I've apologized to each of you for that behavior. But it's a part of me, and I'd be a fool to ignore it or try to bury it. Now, you all have presents and stockings to open, so let's get busy, okay?"

And with that, the Betters family resumed their holiday celebration, exchanging gifts and the occasional loving insult, some even aimed at Franklin, which delighted him, for the last thing he wanted his crew to do was treat him delicately for the rest of his life. Franklin knew owning his mistakes was part of his healing process.

"Hey, Martin," said Franklin as the younger set washed dishes in the kitchen, "you still have that basketball in your car?"

"As a matter of fact, I do," said Martin. "Why do you ask?"

"Well, you never did beat me in H-O-R-S-E," said Franklin. "Feel lucky, punk?"

"Oh, you're on, old man," said Martin.

When they got out to the driveway, Martin was surprised to see the tattered net had been replaced.

"Yep, this was planned, son," said Franklin. "Hope you're ready to lose."

So, the two proceeded to play, missing way more shots than they made—the sun would likely set before either reached even the "R"—but having a wonderful time, nonetheless. The family watched from the window, losing track of missed shots and taking side bets on whether Franklin, Martin, or the sunset would prevail. The sunset was a 3:2 favorite.

And the battered garage door?

A few weeks earlier, Franklin returned Martin's repair check from Thanksgiving, saying, "No, let it stay as is. It still does its job, and it'll remind me that perfection's not all it's cracked up to be. You know, one of our dining-room chairs has an imprint on the back of it from a teething boy, who, unknown to us, was gnawing away at it while his mother was holding him. Every time it catches my eye, it makes me think of that little boy and the fine man he grew up to be. The door stays, Martin."

There was, however, one noticeable difference in the door. The basketball-sized dent, with a little bit of paint and a lot of love, had been transformed into a sunrise, thanks to his granddaughter Michaela.

Meanwhile, a few blocks away, another father and son landed on the same idea. Luca and Vic happily played game after game as an audience of two cats, still wearing their Santa caps, rooted both of them on until they grew tired from their long, happy day and nestled down for a double-decker nap.

THE NEW YEAR ARRIVED with a blast of cold that ended any thought of additional wintertime H-O-R-S-E rematches but afforded Red and Fatty a handy excuse to keep wearing their Christmas caps every waking minute.

Luca returned to school but couldn't wait to get home to get his hands on his new guitar and occasionally was accompanied by Fatty, who, true to her word, sang louder now that Luca was electrified.

One day around lunchtime, Franklin showed up holding a small bag.

"Sorry to bother you when you're working, Vic, but I was doing some grocery shopping, and I got a little something for the cats," he said.

"Oh, not a problem at all, Franklin," said Vic. "I was taking a break, anyway. How was your Christmas?"

"Splendid, Vic. The whole family was there. Everything was perfect. How about you?"

"Great, thanks. Luca got his new guitar, and the cats got their prosciutto."

"Ah, yes, and I figured they might have run out by now, so . . ."

He handed Vic the bag. The cats, hearing every word, appeared in the kitchen and approached the bag.

Franklin chuckled. "They have great senses of smell, don't they?"

"Yep. And how's your four-legged gang these days?"

"Oh, they're wonderful. Sunrise gets a little more pleasant each day, and they all get along great."

"That's nice to hear," said Vic.

"Well, I'll let you get back to work," said Franklin.

"It's always nice seeing you, Franklin," said Vic. "Don't be a stranger."

"I promise you I won't be. And goodbye, Red and Fatty."

As soon as the front door closed, Red began pestering Vic.

"All right, you two. First of all, thank you for being normal for a few minutes while Franklin was here. And yes, you may have some for lunch."

"I'm liking that Franklin more and more each day," said Red. "Let's dig in, Fatty."

"I think I'll skip it for now, if that's okay," said Fatty.

"You sure, buddy?" asked Vic.

"Yes. I'll have some later," said Fatty.

"This is delicious stuff, pal," said Red. "There might not be a later."

"Don't worry, Fatty," said Vic. "Red's not getting all of this. All right, you two. I'm going back to the office. You know where to find me."

As Red was stuffing his face with prosciutto, he stopped midbite, thinking he had come upon a revelation.

"Fatty, did you make a New Year's resolution to lose weight?" he asked.

"No, Red," said Fatty. "I'm just not hungry right now."

Red resumed eating but then looked up. "You know, 'Slightly Less Fatty' isn't nearly as adorable a name."

"Just make sure you save me some, Red. I'm going for a nap," said Fatty.

The week played out as most weeks in January do: You go to school or work in the dark. By 4:00 p.m., it starts to get dark again. In the tight window of daylight you're given, you do your work and your chores, shovel snow when necessary, and feel like going to bed by 6:30 because you're convinced it's at least 10:00 p.m.

One night at bedtime, Fatty made a confession to Red.

"Red, I'm not feeling so great," she said.

"What do you mean?" asked Red.

"I'm—I'm not very hungry. I don't have much energy. I don't know what's wrong."

"Oh, that's why you hardly ate any of the prosciutto Franklin brought over," said Red.

"I'm scared, Red. Please don't tell anyone. Just hold me."

And so, he did. He hugged his friend as hard as he could, and now he was as worried as she was. But when she fell asleep, Red snuck away, because while he didn't want to betray his friend's confidence, he knew Vic and Claudia had to be aware of the situation.

He hopped onto Vic and Claudia's bed and began gently tapping them.

"Papa, Mama," he whispered.

Vic looked at his phone. "It's 2:38 in the morning, Reddy. What do you want?"

"It's Fatty. She told me she doesn't feel right."

Claudia patted Red's head. "We know, dear. She hasn't been eating as much as she normally does. I called the vet the other day. She has an appointment soon."

"Is . . . is she going to be okay?" asked Red.

"It's probably no big deal, Red," said Vic. "Her appointment's in two days. She'll be fine."

"Can you promise me that, Papa?" asked Red.

Vic sighed. "No, Red, I can't promise you that. But think positive thoughts."

"She told me to hold her because she's scared," said Red. "I think it's serious."

"Red, your worrying will do her no good," said Claudia. "Go back to her and be the friend she needs. We'll talk to her in the morning."

Red did as he was told, but he couldn't sleep a wink. And while he knew Claudia was right and that his worrying would do no good, he did so, anyway, all the while staring at his friend and saying a silent prayer on her behalf.

When Fatty awoke, Red informed her that Vic and Claudia already knew she wasn't feeling well.

"But I don't want to go to the vet, Red," said Fatty. "I hate it there."

"Yeah, I know, but maybe they can make you better," said Red.

"Red's right, Fatty," said Vic, who was eavesdropping.

"But, Kind Sir, let me just rest. I'm sure it'll go away on its own, whatever it is."

"Fatty, I know you don't like going to the vet's, but I'll be there with you the whole time," said Vic. "We need to know what's ailing you so we can make you better. Sometimes things don't go away on their own."

Fatty knew Vic was right. "I understand," she said before hopping up to the living-room windowsill.

"You're a good friend for telling us, Red," said Vic.

Red nodded at Vic and nestled down for a nap, seeing how he hadn't slept much the previous night.

The night before Fatty's appointment, nothing felt right. Luca practiced his guitar, but his accompanist didn't feel much like singing. She sat at his feet while he played, hoping the music would make her feel better. Vic and Claudia engaged in small talk, trying to mask how worried they were about their friend. And Red was as subdued as he'd ever been, hardly eating anything himself.

That night, Red held his friend tight again. It helped both of them as they drifted off to sleep, worried what tomorrow would bring but happy that they had each other.

Not having eaten much for several days, Fatty needed some gentle assistance from Vic to get her into the carrier.

"I'll see you soon, pal," said Red, "and in the meantime, I'll think of a way for us to get in trouble."

Vic smiled at Red. "She'll be fine, Red. And we'll be back before you know it."

"Well, Fatty," said Vic, trying to lighten her mood, "the last time we were on our way to the vet, you gave me the surprise of my life. What do you have in store for me this time?"

"Nothing, Kind Sir. I just want this to be over with."

"Fatty, I can't promise you that everything's going to be okay, but I can promise you that you are surrounded by love. Whatever the news is, we're all here for you."

"I know. And I appreciate that."

It wasn't a long trip, but they drove the remainder of the way in silence. Vic knew there was nothing he could say to allay his friend's fears.

"Hello," said Vic upon entering the vet's office. "We're here for Fatty's appointment."

"Of course," said the receptionist. "Please have a seat. We'll be with you shortly."

Vic looked around the waiting area. He knew all the pets there were loved. And all of them were special. But he also knew Fatty possessed a skill set that made her unique. He hoped and prayed for the best, but he feared the worst. The waiting was almost unbearable. Finally . . .

"Hello, Fatty," said Dr. Amoroso. "Follow me, guys."

At least now they would know.

"So, what seems to be the problem?"

"Well," said Vic, "her appetite has been not so great for about a week. She's not eating nearly as much as she normally does. And she seems a bit lethargic."

"Well, let's take her temperature and run some other tests," said the vet, "and we'll go from there. Come on, Fatty. Let's get you into another room."

So, Vic sat by himself for what felt like days. He read through the cat magazines in the room and felt bad every time he saw a cat that reminded him of Fatty. He texted Claudia a few times to tell her what was going on, which wasn't much.

Finally, the doctor returned, and the look on her face told Vic everything he didn't want to hear. She released Fatty from the carrier and unwittingly told both of them the news.

"I'm so sorry, Vic, but she has acute renal failure, which, from the X-rays, appears to have been caused by a tumor. There isn't much we can do for her."

Vic instinctively covered Fatty's ears in a loving, but desperate, attempt to shield his friend from the horrible news.

Dr. Amoroso gently placed her hand atop Vic's and smiled. "You're a kind soul, but don't worry. She can't understand us. Keep her comfortable and be with her. I'll give you a moment, if you'd like. Again, I'm so sorry."

Vic nodded as the doctor departed.

He was doing his best to keep his emotions in check and wanted to do everything he could at that moment to alleviate Fatty's terror.

"You were right, Fatty." he said. "She does have cold hands."

Fatty looked at Vic and nodded. She knew what he was doing, and she was grateful.

"Oh, and, Fatty? You were right about something else, too. When we got him from the shelter, Red's name was Orville."

"I knew it," she said, barely above a whisper.

And then Vic gave his friend, the scaredy cat who was brave and wise and kind too many times to count, the biggest hug he could, and they shared a good cry before composing themselves and heading home.

CLAUDIA, LUCA, AND RED were all waiting for Vic and Fatty to arrive, and a simple head shake from Vic upon entering the house confirmed their worst fears.

"Guys, Fatty is very sick," he began. "She has acute renal failure, which probably came from a tumor."

"What's 'renal,' Dad?" asked Luca.

"Her kidneys, honey," said Claudia.

"But the vet's going to make her better, right, Papa?" asked Red.

Vic sighed. Luca embraced Claudia, who was crying.

"Reddy, there's nothing they can do. It's an advanced illness."

Red ran out of the room.

Fatty went after him.

The three humans embraced, all crying, unsure what to say.

Sure, Vic and Claudia had buried a lot of pets in their lives, but none of them talked or were so intertwined in the day-to-day activities of their household. This was different. This hurt in ways they couldn't imagine.

"Red," said Fatty. "Stop."

"No. I want to be alone. This is like saying goodbye to Mom, but it's worse because at least there was always a chance I'd see her again."

Fatty patted Red's cheek. It was wet.

"I love you, Reddy Redson. You're my best friend."

"I . . . I love you, too, Fatty. You can't leave us."

"I guess that's not for me to decide," said Fatty.

That night, they embraced tighter than ever. Fatty was afraid, but Vic's words from the car ride echoed in her brain, and she knew that indeed she was surrounded by love—in Red's case, quite literally.

The next day, Vic and Claudia pulled Luca and Red aside while Fatty was napping and told them that the best thing they all could do was put on a brave face for their friend. There would be no crying in front of her. Spend time with her. Make her laugh. Act normal around her.

And that's what they did.

Red was constantly by her side, never showing her how his little heart was being shattered. Luca made sure she was nearby every time he practiced his guitar. It seemed to soothe her. Aurora visited as often as she could. And Claudia and Vic spent extra time with her. She was never alone.

But when Vic and Claudia were alone, they found themselves overwhelmed by melancholy. Vic repeatedly played back the videos he took of Red and Fatty and would laugh through his tears at the one where Red was terrified to discover that Fatty ate animals when she was living outside.

He was playing back the cats' Christmas present when Claudia walked in . . .

'Cause it's Christmas, Christmas
And our love is sincere

"You're torturing yourself, babe," said Claudia.

"Do you have any better ideas?" said Vic.

She shook her head and watched along with Vic. It was only three weeks ago that Fatty was her happiest self, singing a Christmas song made especially for them, with not a care in the world. It didn't seem fair.

"She always knew what to say, you know?" said Claudia.

"We're all better for having known her," said Vic.

"But we needed to know her way longer," said Luca, who was just as sad as his parents.

"I loved it when she sang," he said. "She was so funny. And she always felt so bad when I would end up in trouble because of her and Red."

As the days progressed, Fatty grew weaker. All they could do was make sure she was resting comfortably. They all knew the end was near, and Red almost never left her side.

The family gathered around her after dinner, and Vic wanted to say a few words while Fatty could still hear them.

"It was our great fortune to know you, Fatty," he said. "But, dang it, we didn't know our time with you would be so short. We love you. We will always love you. And we will all cherish the time we spent with you. You were kind. And funny. And brave. And wise."

His voice started to break, but he soldiered on.

"You touched all of us in your own special way. You made us all better beings. And what you did for Franklin changed the course of his life. I don't know why you're being taken from us, but your time here was well-spent and special and full of meaning. You will never be forgotten, friend."

And amid a roomful of tears, a very quiet "I love all of you" could be heard.

Fatty fought on for a few more days, but one day after dinner, Red came running into the kitchen.

"Guys" was all he said. They knew.

Instinctively, they each lay a hand or paw on her. She was gone now, but they knew her goodness would impact and influence all their lives as they moved forward without her. She would be a part of all their stories, and the brief time she spent with them would forever place a smile on their hearts.

A knock at the door.

Vic motioned to answer it, but Claudia tried to stop him. "We can ignore it," she said.

"It might be important, honey," he said.

He cleared his throat as he approached the door, trying to regain his composure.

Vic opened the door, saw nothing, then almost passed out.

"Nine lives, Kind Sir."

It was Fatty, looking like her old, wonderful, chubby, healthy self.

"But—but that's just a myth."

"I'm a talking cat, K.S. I'm full of surprises."

And through the happiest of tears, Vic, Claudia, and Luca embraced and found themselves jumping in unison, as if they had just won the World Series, as if they had just won every World Series ever played.

And Red?

He felt the urgent need to show off again for his best pal, so he dashed from the kitchen, tore through the dining room, and landed gracefully atop the living-room bookshelf.

After all, you never know when a gazelle might show up.